The Rest is Silence

by

James Patrick

2nd Edition
(21st October 2012)
© 2012 James Patrick.
ISBN 978-1-300-25463-8

First published 7th October 2012.

Cover Art - 'PFTP' Logo by 'Dave'
http://www.dave-artspot.blogspot.co.uk

Acknowledgements:

This publication is based upon my blogs, which were in the public domain for weeks and months. Subsequently they have been available for open comment, debate and suggested revision. The blogs have been read by over 40,000 people and have proven popular and free of complaint. Almost all were originally written on a mobile telephone.

A lot of public access material is referenced throughout and I would like to offer a public thanks to all of those I have, already very openly, linked or attributed
material to.

Should you wish to get in touch now, you can do so via:

thedutytank@gmail.com
www.twitter.com/j_amesp
or, via comments at:
www.thepolicedebatingdirective.blogspot.com

You will find the online appendices at the blog, listed under the title of this book. Where a relevant link exists, it is shown by a bold, underlined number, within this text.

Special thanks to SS for proofreading and MK McMullen for the rapid and complete edit of this second edition. A third will follow.

Author's Note:

There are many people who I have to thank.
Some for their sore thumbs, others for laughter,
some for challenging me to be better and all,
for constant support and companionship.
You've kept me going and you know who you
are. If, on the other hand, you've never read me
before, you need to know that I write as I
speak; using the semicolon to replicate a short
breath between statements.

For every copy of this sold, a donation will be
made to the charity Care of Police Survivors
(www.ukcops.org), who do quite wonderful
work, helping rebuild the lives of families,
shattered by the loss of life, in the line of duty. I
might not be able to do much, in the grand
scheme of things but; I can do that.

Throughout this I've been flying by the seat of
my pants, sailing close to the wind and; doing it
without a safety net. No sanction, no debrief.
My career, as a serving police officer, has been
at risk at every step and, one day this may bite
me. Whatever happens, I've done it for you;
despite the fact that, in most cases, we've never
even heard of each other. I hope that counts for
something.

JP.

*"They shall not grow old, as we are that are
left to grow old.*

*Age shall not weary them, not the years
condemn.*

*At the going down of the sun and in the
morning*

We will remember them"

For the Fallen.

Laurence Binyon (1914)

The Obligatory Foreword:

"There is no point blindly plodding along, accepting everything at face value"

The first ever blog I posted to "The Police Debating Directive" was not, as such, a blog. It was a letter.

At the time I had an overview of the coming reforms to policing, gained through official publications, but had no real idea what I was going to be finding out over the coming months. In my innocence, I suppose, I was thinking of what Lord Nelson said at the battle of Trafalgar in 1805:

"England expects that every man will do his duty".

At the time I saw my duty as to ask for help from the very person I am sworn to serve. So, to begin at the beginning, as is invariably the best place to start; I wrote to Our Sovereign Lady, HM The Queen. It does come across a bit floral in patches but, I assure you, I did read the official guidelines on the Monarchy website before committing pen to paper. As of yet, I have received no reply; yet I live with a glass that remains half full and, despite everything I now know, an irritatingly cheerful belief that, somehow, this will all 'turn out alright'.

The background to how I came to write *The Last Call to Attention* is really quite mundane. It had been pretty cold through the winter, me trudging to and from shifts. Leaving my house at 4am for early shifts, 11.30am for late shifts and 7pm for nights; crawling home, or back into bed, at 7pm for early shifts, between 1am and 6am for late shifts and 10am for nights. If I got back home at all. A lot of my life was being spent on a train or, on a rail replacement bus service. I was tired. I was exhausted. Around me, I was the only one on top of what was happening in the world of police reform. I was the font of all knowledge, a fortune teller. I was Mystic Meg.

All the while the realisation dawned. I had never, not in my service, heard a decent speech, a proper one, from any police leader and, with almost cast iron certainty, none would be forthcoming. So, I decided to write my own. To imagine what I would say, if it was me at the helm. It may not be perfect. It may not make me Winston Churchill but; it meant something to me and, with the help of Youtube, Twitter, Sir Ian Blair (the spoof), Inspector Gadget and my rather vocal, nine month old daughter, it meant something to around 15,000 others too.

Having made the video, which at this point had begun to circulate at quite a pace and, having been told that it had been discussed at quite a senior level; I started to notice a common theme emerging in the world of Twitter and, in the mainstream media. It seemed that the fact that police officers are also human beings, had been left well out of all discussions and coverage of police reforms. I desperately wanted to try and explain the nuts and bolts of it, to make people who weren't police officers aware of the wider impact of the coming reform. If only just for a moment.

What I arrived at, on a late, late train ride home from a gruelling day, was my first real effort at engaging with members of the public. What I didn't know then is how absolutely crucial that just talking openly to all people, about what it actually means to be a police officer, was going to be. It's very easy for us coppers to get lost in our own little niche. To assume that people really understand what it is we do, how that changes us and our lives. I have been as guilty of that at times as many, many others. I see it in my own blogs, as will you too; at first I was speaking predominantly to other police officers. I for one am glad I realised this relatively early on in this adventure.

On the 17th of April a kerfuffle broke out. The Police Federation had announced a mass march, in London, on the 10th of May. The problem arose because other unions, the PCS, Unite and others if I recall correctly, would also be marching that day. It may seem hard to understand the friction that this caused, why it resulted in some police officers even launching into tirades against PCSOs. The reason behind it is quite simply that coppers have no industrial rights, so any marches must be organised and carried out in free time. The impact of other unions taking action on the same day was, quite simply, an increased likelihood that officers would have days off cancelled or leave restricted, thus potentially reducing the number of officers able to carry out the only kind of action they are allowed to. I actually saw it as an opportunity, a chance, to make sure people really understood that particular issue. Maybe even to get some support, on behalf of the officers that wouldn't be able to attend. It was beyond my power to stop any divisions being opened up, that could potentially cause the police further damage in the long run, but I thought I'd try. The emergency services should always stand together.

I'd never really been involved in any kind of group, movement or activism before but, I suppose, I became part of something. I still don't really know what! This dawned on me when Occupy Police, based in the US, picked up the Youtube video and posted it on their web site. I felt a bit rebellious when this happened, like a naughty school kid, but really I just thought "crikey, now there's a breakthrough". You see, if an international movement like Occupy, very often pitched against the police, could see something that we could all work towards, legally, ethically, peacefully; then, maybe, something really special could happen. Aside from this, my closest encounter with any kind of protest (from a not on duty perspective) was in San Francisco, in March 2004, where I stumbled into a million man march, against the war in Iraq. At the Civic Centre, on the day I was due to leave, I immersed myself in a huge crowd and took some amazing photographs. I will always remember a group dressed as boxes walking past, an old Bob Dylan tune playing somewhere in the crowd. Two months later I was a police officer.

So if you ever wonder where the phrase: "I police the 100%, I am the 99%, I do not fear the 1%" first came from. It was me.

As the day of what would be the largest police march in recent history loomed, as the start of my eighth year as a copper was due to occur on the same day; I turned my thoughts to how we, really, could be facing the last days of Peelian policing. For me it was absolutely essential that, if we were fighting for something, we had to be fighting for the right something. We couldn't just go forwards preserving the status quo and keeping things as they were.

The march went well, my policing anniversary came and went and, for the first time, I saw a proper head to head debate between the Crime and Justice Minister, Nick Herbert and the head of the Police Federation, Paul McKeever. I was hugely interested to see how this would go but, at the same time, I didn't want to take a one sided view of it. In the most detached way I could and, knowing that this might upset some people, I wrote the most balanced account of it that I could muster. The response to this was, as I predicted, quite flat to say the least. But...and there is a but; if you approach anything from a completely one sided view, you can rarely achieve anything and, can miss any opportunities that present themselves.

Almost two months after I first started plugging away, the HASC were due to hold a hearing, to talk to Nick Herbert and Tom Winsor, about the police reform agenda. Like many others I took the opportunity to write to the Chairman, the Rt Hon Keith Vaz, to express my concerns. I remember feeling almost euphoric that this hearing was coming. It felt like a triumph, as if there was some final light, at the end of what was starting to look like a very long tunnel. With infinite hope and belief in the system, I wrote an open email to the Chair.

To my absolute surprise (and if I'm totally honest, delight) I found that this email was included in an article in *The New Statesman*, with a direct link to the blog. I may be paraphrasing but, I'm sure the author of the article called this email 'one of the more interesting items' he had found on the topic. The fact that someone found what I had to say interesting, not least of someone who writes articles for a living...well that was nice.

By June, I was deeply researching every single aspect of the proposed police reforms and the thing which had been niggling at me for quite some time was Police and Crime Commissioners (PCCs). Not the candidates themselves, some of them are pretty pleasant, but the whole set up. To me, saying that you are cutting 20% from an emergency service budget and then spending £100 million on a new layer of politicians, is just daft. My concerns on the way it would work, the dangers of it, had been mounting and then, an event was held by my new favourite think tank, The Policy Exchange. The event was attended by Nick Herbert, amongst others, sponsored no less, by Deloitte (who stand to be doing quite a lot of consultancy I would imagine). What came out of it did very little, other than to compound exactly what I had thought all along. After the PCC event I decided it was time to write to one of the organ grinders. I can't remember what I was doing at the time but I can say with some certainty that I will have smoked many cigarettes and drank at least one latte.

The only other thing I will say, about my letters to the minister, is that I don't beat around the bush. I had already learned enough, to make every single one of my alarm bells sing as loudly as a drunken, karaoke chorus.

In particular on Twitter, a lot of police officers and former police officers use anonymity. I know the reasons why, I can fully understand it. Police stations (and now the newspapers) are littered with tales of Bobbies who have fallen foul of social media. Me? Well, from the moment I decided to make that letter HM The Queen public, especially since Youtube, I figured, for me anonymity wasn't my bag. The whole point is choice. So, when someone that I respect started to get a lot of grief from corporate Tweeters, about their own choice to be anonymous, with an undertone of exposing them against their wishes; I thought I'd say something about it. It's an unusual thing, to hear a police officer singing the praises of the Human Rights Act but, when you know what it actually means, what it is actually for: then, you can't help but want to uphold it.

Tom Winsor was then appointed the new Chief Inspector of Constabularies. Not only that but, at his hearing at the Home Affairs Select Committee, it transpired that he had never claimed the money he had been offered for his review. It also occurred that tweeting police officers, who had used the hash tag #AntiWinsorNetwork (including myself), were called names by Nick Herbert. I yawned at this spin. Because that was all it was. I did however take a lesson from Nick Herbert on this: play the ball, not the man.

A new month then started, July. I pinched and punched and knuckled down and; the dirt started to flow. Around this time, the hash tag #PFTP had already taken off. It's double meaning absolutely perfect: Police For The Public / Public For The Police. With renewed vigour, new ground was broken. I focused squarely on the dangers of privatisation and, in this, the biggest swinger in the jungle: G4S. This was before it became an official, Olympic sized problem. Then, when the story broke, the blog actually got used as source material for some national news.

I suppose all I have ever wanted, is for people to talk about what is happening, to debate issues and potential problems. There is no point blindly plodding along, accepting everything at face value. Public safety is much too important for that kind of approach and, as I often say, policing is not a tickling competition; not a game.

As the old Cicero saying goes "The safety of the public shall be the highest law".

Hold that thought.

Open Letter - HM The Queen:

"I have sacrificed my rights in order to serve"

9th of April 2012

Dear Madam,

I say, with a great deal of pride, that in May I will have served in the sworn office of Constable for 8 years.

In that time I have been bruised, battered, attacked with a knife, bled upon, spat at, racially abused, threatened, had my home address sold in exchange for drugs, arrested countless criminals, been subject to the attentions of corrupt and selfish police officers, missed a huge amount of meals and, more importantly, a large amount of time with my wife and my young children. I have had no control over my working pattern and no guarantees of days off, sleeping an average of five hours or less between shifts. I have sacrificed my rights in order to serve; a conscious choice in a society that teaches us against it.

I have taken on the undisciplined, the selfish and the corrupt within the service - no matter what level of service or rank they may have attained. I have seen first hand what happens; what human nature makes people capable of, when they see someone take a stand without fear of them. I have spent time with those that many would not pass the time with; I have bought hot coffee for prostitutes on the coldest of nights, I have sat and drawn up house rules with the care home children that have been abused within their families and are labelled too difficult to be 'saved' by care workers. I have seen people, that I knew as a child, wrecked and ruined by the use of heroin and crack cocaine.

I have seen some of the most horrific and haunting sights. I have stared into the eyes of the dying and the lifeless, choking down my own physical and involuntary reactions; all the while preserving my nerve and my emotions, then going home with those experiences engrained upon me, the faces and sights I will never forget and, for better or worse, have to carry this alone as my dinner table is no place for such discussion.

I have made a difference, to victimised individuals, to bereaved and suffering families, to victims and suspects alike. I have had the privilege to work with whole communities and have delivered long term improvements in the quality of their lives, through reducing crime, through tackling drugs; through supporting the troubled, young and old.

Despite all of this, in spite of all of this; because of all of this, I would not change a single moment from the evening in which I swore my oath of attestation. I have kept and will forever keep my promise to Your Majesty, Our Sovereign Lady and to all of your servants.

I look around however and see the Police Service, in chaos; despair. Apathy. We have lost our way and many, through example of both policy and leadership, are content to exist in a system that no more serves Your Majesty, than it does the public we are sworn to protect. Those of us who do not serve only our own interests will continue to do our duty, no matter what is thrown at us, whether it be by the outside world or by our peers. Those of us who do not only serve ourselves are the light within the Police Service, a light that must not be extinguished; for once it is finally snuffed, a tipping point will be reached. A point which, once reached, will begin an unstoppable process, whereby the proud traditions of policing by consent will no longer have a place in British society; whereby any oath sworn will mean nothing. Where the misinterpreted and abused cultures of targets, that have caused such damage already, will be replaced by a much more insatiable appetite; by greed, personal advantage and, inevitably, by corruption on many new levels. The green shoots of this are already, clearly, visible and we are not yet at the brink. Worse will come.

The Police must be reformed! But, at the same time, this reform must come from real leaders, from those who will put themselves second, who refuse to talk in riddles, who will not accept nonsense, who will be honest; even when the truth is not palatable. It is a sad day indeed when, having served, having done everything you can, you come to the realisation that what lies around you is smoke and mirrors, a dangerous illusion. A selfish, self contained, self promoted reality; barely held within a tight blue circle of misplaced honour and loyalty; of deceit. The service does lie, both to itself and the public and until we acknowledge this we will continue to edge closer to the tipping point; until we stand firm and declare the truth and that the truth hurts, nothing can change for the better.

I am not writing to Your Majesty for interference in matters of pay and conditions, as a loyal servant I will accept whatever financial fate awaits me; it is a matter for Government, beyond my own control and Your Majesty's proper sphere of influence. I do however, for the first and last time, break from subservience to pose a question.

Madam, I am your sworn servant and, now more than ever we need to lead the Police Service out of a confused identity crisis, to once again make it a force to be reckoned with; to be proud to be part of it and to have the full support of those we serve. We do not lack a figurehead but the memory of it, of what we are here to do, has become increasingly hazy. Distant.

Your Majesty, you are that figurehead and we need you. We need to hear your rallying cry. We need to be reminded of who we are, of our promises; of our purpose. I respectfully request that, in your Jubilee year, you consider this letter Your Majesty and, if you see fit, publicly issue such a call. The good amongst us, the selfless and the dedicated will reply.

Whenever that call may come; we are waiting and ready to raise the roof. I have the honour to be, Madam, Your Majesty's humble and obedient servant.

The Last Call to Attention:

"We remain the sworn few; we are the calm before, during and after the storm"

13th of April 2012

Our boots may be worn, our finances stretched both in our forces and in our households; but we remain the sworn few.

We are the thinnest blue line, our morale frayed, our discipline time-eroded and our good will stretched well beyond where it should have snapped; but we remain the sworn few.

Judged daily on our appearance, on how we dress and on the faith we have, the faith in our promise to society and ourselves; we know prejudice first hand.

Even under direct attack, the physical, the mental, and the written. The accidental, circumstantial and deliberate; we must not fall into the traps laid down. We remain the sworn few; we are the calm before, during and after the storm.

Facing the highest level of danger and often the lowest levels of common sense; while the will of many falters and, as the skeletons gather dust, unseen in even the highest of closets; we remain the sworn few.

We put ourselves second, third. Fourth. In

doing so, choosing not to join the clubs that exist; to work without the safety networks many hide within and behind. We will never sell out, never sell our souls; a difficult path indeed.

The biggest threat to us has always been self interest. The wide, open door to corruption, paths of least resistance; to the imposition of personal prejudice. We rise above this, the sworn few.

We are the voiceless, by choice, surrendering our rights to walk this path; an understated, misunderstood and abused sacrifice. When those who taunt us expect anger and noise, we must give them nothing; silence, dignity and discipline. Our strongest possible response. The eeriest and most unnerving reply.

We the sworn few, who gave away our voices are now, too, speechless. How much will it take to make us not care; to no longer try? More than they have. We will simply do as we promised and, in doing so, turn our cheeks. United we stand behind the oaths that bind us.

We are portrayed as the least equal of all animals, yet we see the glimmers behind the exteriors; we personally know the dangers of fractions of fractions. We see first hand the effects of agenda, half truth and blatant, statistical manipulation. We the sworn few must stand tall. We must stand together.

Within our ranks there is no space for the bigoted, ineffective, corrupt; not in any of their many disguises. We have no space for them as we stand, this last time, shoulder to shoulder; as the world around us is shaken, to its very foundations.

Rarely do we hear the rallying cries that are desperately needed; so with this, from a humble holder of the Office of Constable, from our very own coalface: join me, the sworn few. Join me in one last call to attention; one last stand of dignity and discipline in the face of adversity.

Stand side-by-side and stand proud.

Let us shout together and, from the basements, pavements, tower blocks and roof tops, let us remind Great Britain who we truly are.

Stand with me, the sworn few and let our oath, our promise, the strong words that bind us resound in every street. Every alleyway and every police station that remains. Join me and show every person, in every estate, village, town and city, that we are here, for each and every one of them; we do as we must, in spite of the personal consequences, of the obstacles, the dangers and the pressures. The last guardians of morality.

Together, let us make a thunder that cannot be ignored, a renewed pride that cannot be extinguished; let the whole country echo and let the corridors of power shake with those words that begin this journey, for each and every one of us.

Join me and, maybe for the last time, let's raise the roof:

"I do solemnly and sincerely declare and affirm that I will well and truly serve Our Sovereign Lady the Queen in the office of Constable, without favour or affection, malice or ill will; and that I will to the best of my power cause the peace to be kept and preserved and prevent all offences against the persons and properties of Her Majesty's subjects; and that while I continue to hold the said office I will to the best of my skill and knowledge discharge all the duties thereof, faithfully and according to the law."

The Price of a Soul:

"What is your price to carry the faces of the dead, the touch of their skin, the feel of the knot"

17th of April 2012

What is your price? What value do you put,
would you put without being pressed, upon
your own life?

How much to go toe-to-toe, to grapple with the
person spitting Hepatitis into your nose, eyes.
Mouth. Sometimes that person will bleed,
maybe the HIV virus. Sometimes a Tubercular
cough; maybe reckless but often with malice,
purpose. In the heat of that moment of hatred.

What cost to stand with the person, their
psychotic break complete, armed with glass, a
hammer; knives. Just you and them, alone in
the dark. You unarmed; limbs, head, throat, face
– exposed to the cruel implements glinting
before you. You unarmed; mentally choosing
which piece of you to sacrifice, what you can
live with, or without. Which piece of you, if
lost or wounded, will impact the least on your
ability to disarm, to arrest; to use your radio to
make, possibly, your final call for help. How
many pieces of silver to make this choice and
keep your head; decisions cool, reactions
tempered.

What is it worth to live on five hours sleep,
often less; to sneak into your own home, in the
middle of the night. Creeping like the midnight

thief you constantly keep in your sights; leaving
again before your family, your loved ones, even
know you were there at all. How much for you
to become the phantom of your home life; the
ghost partner, husband, wife, father, mother,
brother, sister; son or daughter.

What is your price to carry the faces of the
dead, the touch of their skin, the feel of the
knot. The cries and screams of the injured; the
tears of the children who...

What value on the sacrifice of thirty years of
your life, three decades to do all of this and
more; to only do the right thing by others,
whom often you will never see more than one
time. To put your identity in second place. To
surrender the rights you take for granted,
choice; privacy. To give them away while
defending those of strangers.

How much to put yourself under the
unwavering lens of a microscope. To lay under
the watchful eyes of vultures; made lame by
your own promise and the rules and obligations
that form part of the package.

I chose this, I weighed it up; my eyes were
open. My price was the security that, in thirty
years, having paid a higher share than any

other, having wrecked my health through ever changing shifts, missed sleep; unhealthy, as-and-when eating patterns. Having missed some of the most glorious moments in marriage, in fatherhood; having done some genuine good, having made a real difference: that at the end of three decades, I would be able to be me, the person I put on pause for all that time. Just me; for at least ten years, before finally checking out. The thirty year target, the fixed date; the light at the end of a very dark and very bleak tunnel.

Ask yourselves, what price to stand, walk and run in my shoes? What worth, honestly, do you place upon yourselves? If, genuinely, your answer is that you would do it for longer and for less, well; you are welcome to it. Just remember, none of it is optional; all of it your duty. No excuses, no fear.

When it is all over, will you regret not having enough time to learn how to be 'normal' again; will you regret spending each day waiting for your broken heart and battered body to give out? Will you regret putting your family through this, their own lives equally impacted by the choice you made; are you willing to risk the collapse of those relationships, every time you call to say you can't come home?

I'm a Police Officer, your servant; do with me as you will. All I ask is that, in doing so, you think about it; about what it means. Nothing more, nothing less. Ask yourselves; what is your price? What value do you put on your family? What value your life? Ask yourselves: What value do you put on mine?

Never Feed the Hungry Crocodile:

"We are either all in, with each other and for each other; or we are done"

18th of April 2012

Yesterday; anger, upset. Division. Have we become so used to attack that we see it, even in those who would walk with us? In those who make up the very lines we are trying to hold? Calm. Seek the opportunity in the difficulty; for there is one.

Unite. For we must learn to walk together, or we risk the fate of the fool; we will be the divided house that perishes. A divided house, as said Abraham Lincoln, cannot stand.

Coming together to hold the line is our beginning. Keeping that line strong will be our only road to progress. Only holding that line together, can we succeed.

We must never let the overt tactic of divide and conquer rule; never allow ourselves to become disaffected, downhearted. There is always a way. Whether Police Officer, Doctor, Nurse, Teacher, Civil Servant or Administrator. Tinker, tailor, soldier or spy; we either hold the line together or accept division. Accept defeat.

On the 10th of May 2012 we are either all in, with each other, for each other; or we prove our portrayal as the selfish, greedy, gold-plated, inflexible and ineffective. We are either all in, with each other and for each other; or we are done. Being united is our exigency; our urgent and pressing need.

As Police Officers we are ever losing numbers; if there aren't enough of us left, so as to make it necessary cancel leave and rest days: our point is well made. The picture complete. As Police Officers we are sworn to protect the rights of others; their freedom of expression, freedom of thought, freedom of conscience. But, our historic tradition tells us clearly; the police are the public and the public are the police. We are simply paid to give full time attention to the obligations of all citizens.

So Doctors, Nurses, Tinkers, Tailors; will you fulfil your obligations and stand for those who cannot? All of you, your Unions; PCS, Unite, Unison: will, on the 10th of May 2012, you safeguard the rights of others; of us? Doing this, so they say is the most beautiful act a human being can carry out. If we cannot be there because our oath prevents it, because duty has called. Because obligation makes it so; will you stand for us? We are you and you, us. Would you carry the message; the police can't be here because we are? Would you remind all you see; having rights means exercising your own AND doing so on behalf of those who can't?

If we stand against each other now, in these hardest of times, all of our voices will be lost; our entwined fates sealed by the noise of our division. If we stand together, stand with and for each other, our voice will be so loud, so powerful; it will echo around the world.

The choice we make, the path we take on the 10th of May 2012 will decide all of our futures. The futures of our families; the futures of the very institutions we all dedicate ourselves to.

As a child I was taught two very important lessons.

1) Never cut your nose off to spite your face and;
2) Never feed a hungry crocodile.

To make war with each other over a day, rather than stand with and for each other; to make that division clear and angry, is no better than slicing off our noses. To make this war, to become angry, bitter, divided; would do nothing more than feed the crocodile.

We can either be united, stand united and walk united, or; be divided, stand against each other, walk away from each other. Backs turned for now and forever. If we choose the latter, each and everyone one of us, will inevitably fall.

The Times, They Need Changing:

"To live in a culture of fear, the very thing we fight against for others every day, is a sad and bitter reality indeed"

27th April 2012

Bob Dylan, some years ago, quite aptly
summed up the world we see around us now.

"Come gather round people, wherever you
roam; and admit that the waters around you
have grown. And accept it that soon you'll be
drenched to the bone. If your time to you is
worth saving, then you better start swimming,
or you'll sink like a stone. For the times they are
a changing".

I never understood Dylan as a child; even my
father, a man who I hold in the highest regard,
didn't understand him until much later in life.

I understand him now, Bob Dylan, at least for
the relevance I see as to what is happening to
that thing I love. Being a copper; being
privileged to stand as one of the sworn few.

In less than a month we will gather, in our own
time and without industrial voice, for what it is
worth. We will gather from all over the country,
alongside our families and alongside many
colleagues from other walks in the public
sector.

We are set to walk together as the softest of all
targets, most of us resigned to the fate of the
Winsor reforms. To the savings that will come
from our pockets; from the mouths of our loved

ones. The majority seem to see futility and, sadly, accept it. Personally, I think the police are worth saving. I will not accept that we are only going to march, to get drenched to our bones.

Personally I think there is a way. Oh, I know there is a way and it is not going to be pretty, not going to be easy; not a soft option. But then, while we may be soft targets from a financial perspective, we are hard; physically, mentally, emotionally. Each of us makes life changing decisions, daily. There is no-one better qualified to walk the most difficult path than a Police Officer. A British Police Officer.

For a long time we, the rank and file have been vocal, or at least tried to be. Using everything from encounters with the public, the press, blogs, to express all that is wrong about what we do; the twisted system in which we have to operate.

Traditionally the problem is, or has largely seemed to be, individuals. Often without sanction or official, open backing. Such is the fear of our own culture that the vast majority, even now, will only speak anonymously for fear of being sought out. Even when they are being honest, blowing their whistles in the only way they feel they can; they will be sought out. To live in a culture of fear, the very thing we fight against for others every day, is a sad and bitter reality indeed.

By the very virtue of what we do and the restrictions placed upon us, we have had no real choice, limited opportunity; our roads have been blocked by the continuous storms. Bribery, corruption. Racism. It is astounding, that only a fractional number of individuals, acting badly, wrongly, corruptly, have been able to influence, by their choices, actions and inactions; the entire path of a vast institution. Those few have created so much noise that the rest have been, almost completely, filtered out; rendered further voiceless. Because of this, the vocal few, the good individuals speaking out, are very effectively drowned out; smothered. Or, often reduced to providers of harmless, pulp titillation.

Against this backdrop, amidst this noise, a huge amount of virtually silent change has been effected, driven through. Often passing unnoticed until, that is, somebody realises that there are too many forms keeping officers off the streets, too large and problematic a target culture; not enough response officers to keep the wheels turning smoothly. Not enough police officers on duty, or able to be recalled from rest; to respond to mass events without a critical time lapse.

Within the silent machine there are those who grease the mechanisms, to keep it quiet. These are the unseen and oddly titled roles that have been prolific in their creation, distribution and their influence.

I put my name, my face, to my oath; to The Last Call to Attention, because they are words that, in my whole service, I have never heard. They are exactly the kind of words I have been waiting for and expected someone to deliver. I wanted to know if there were others out there, that still felt like me or, conversely, if it was time to move on. To surrender my warrant and leave, what is apparently perceived to be, a sinking ship behind. The response has gone a long way to reassure me that there is still a glimmer of hope, that there are enough people who still believe in their service; who feel as I do. The response has also confirmed what I know. That I will be sought out.

More importantly, the response has confirmed that officers the length and breadth of the country are at the end of their tethers; being pushed to and beyond their limits but, they will not back down. Together to the bitter end, united.

The police service, our historic tradition, is on the brink; a knife's edge. We now face a crossroads. We can either wait for the waters to claim us, wait to sink like stones, or we can swim. What is important, crucial, if we are to survive is that we swim together and, herein, lies the problem; the bulk of the stones that weight our pockets: not all of us will swim. There are many who would just as happily stand on our shoulders and force us to drown, while they save themselves. These are the silent machine greasers; and those who aspire to their positions. These may be the people that preoccupy themselves with the reclassification of offences to avoid poor performance figures; these may be the people who show team strengths in their forties when in reality; there are only teens on the street. These may be the people who abuse working time regulations as 'guidelines' to avoid displays of their own failings. These may be the people who base major decisions on flawed, or manipulated data.

These may be the people who are blessed with protection from scrutiny under the mask of Direction and Control issues. All of this has become anecdotal in police stations across the land. A cause of much cynicism and is neither unknown, unreported nor too controversial to be said again.

Despite this, the times are changing and if we, the sworn few, swim now and swim together; we stand a chance. We should not however leave any of these people behind to fend for themselves in the deepening waters. Even having pulled them down from our shoulders; sore from bearing their weight. We will do as we are trained to, deal with the immediate risk first and haul them to safety. Then, in the calm that follows the inevitable storm, we will present our evidence and make sure that, where there is an apparent case to answer, they are held to account. We will not however judge them, that is not for us; we are not here to usurp the judiciary.

I advocate that we forgive these people, for their weaknesses and for their mistakes; their conscious choices and sometimes unintended consequences. And, unlike many of them, while we will never forget; in twenty years time they will not find us exacting some vindictive revenge. I have experienced, first hand, that people in this job have long memories; the very phrase a threat, often wielded when challenges to them are made. I have never been swayed by it; not even when they have made good on their words.

The time has come for all of us, as I have said, as we all say; to join together. Join to give a true reflection of the service; not only the positive, but the negative too. Without fear of being sought out, without blind affection. Without any malice or ill will. We must be honest, brutal; free of smoke blowing and lip service.

This is the only way we can swim, the only way we can go against the swell; the tides created out of our hands and above our heads. Collectively we must absolutely dispel all of the smoke and mirrors myths that exist; that have been presented. We must give a true account of what is right and what is wrong within the service. We must do this publicly and to an appropriate audience.

If we do not do this, we must accept the rationale of privatisation. We must accept that the very reason it has come about is because the poor architects and machine greasers have effectively been allowed to build something so unstable, so ill, so dangerous; that the only perceivable way of dealing with it, is to destroy it. This is the proverbial nail being banged on the head. Of all of this, the most terrifying fact is that those very architects of this doomed creation; could be those making the easiest transfers to the private sector replacement.

We, together, have one chance to end this; for with the end of it comes the possibility of real reform. With it comes the real understanding that makes workforce and salary change moot; pointless. Obsolete. This one time; we have the voice and enough of the harmony to make our message heard above all background noise. We are, for now, fearless.

This opportunity, our opportunity, will be fleeting, the smallest of all possible windows. But, if we hit that window, just right, with the full force of a hurricane; we will be able to tear the house down.

I have no fear in calling for an emergency hearing to talk about policing; true policing. About what is wrong with operational policing. About what reform is actually needed. I have no fear of asking others to join me there; others who have proven themselves as worthy holders and former holders of the Office of Constable. I have no fear in asking each one of you to provide one example of something right and something wrong. I say this loud and clear, this is only about doing the right thing by the public that we serve; we are them and they us. We deserve it, they deserve it. A police service that works; no more silent change, no more piecemeal, reactionary antics. A police service that is truly reformed, once and for all.

My call is for a full inquiry, into policing and police reform. Immediate, comprehensive and most importantly; open. Transparent.

My only question is:
Would all in favour of me making that call say Aye?

A Sorry State of Reform:

"a smoke and mirrors idea to trick the public into
believing more cops are about"

30th April 2012

I am tired and on a train. This will not be my best writing but the point is clear.

At a time of unprecedented austerity measures, of 20% police budget cuts and reducing officer numbers. With reports of robbery and knife crime rising; mass potential for civil unrest, the good will of front line police officers stretched by Winsor (pay review) and Hutton (pensions). Amidst a massive need for increased police efficiency at peak times (evenings and nights); a need to get cops out of office and on the street to rebuild community trust; what does the Home Secretary do?

Well, first: ratifies a 10% increase in the cost of policing between 2000 & 0600; our peak time. This is madness! It shows no understanding of police operational business and actively encourages a nine to five culture; it means that chiefs will have to put financials first, especially in the current climate and, have no choice but to consider running less cops at the busiest times. That can only increase danger; this can only increase the risk to those who give up their rights to protect everyone else's. But don't be overly worried for front line cops, they'll be protected! It is okay because the Police Federation have statutory input. They have to agree shifts, considering factors like operational safety...NO.

No, because: secondly the Home Secretary ratifies that chiefs can change patterns on 30 days notice with 'consultation' rather than agreement, meaning that financial impact WILL become a key driving factor. THE key driving factor; with that pesky Federation obstacle removed. This simple one-two combo shows that the process isn't about reforming the police, or rewarding the x factor, but about rubber stamping a service that puts cash before safety of officers and public alike. Almost like a private...oh yeah!

They know this, up in the corridors, away from the street. They know this and they know that we know. Which is why they then turn to think tanks. They know there will be a lack of cops when they are most needed and they need *'public perception solutions'*. So how's about cops travel from home in uniform? That'll increase visibility around shift starts and end times. We could make arguments about safety of families, could say that it will cost forces thousands per head to secure homes, install secure lockers, secure computers and temp property stores; in case crime reports and evidential items are collected on the way home...

We won't do that though; we will just say that it means: with police regulations and working time regs applied, cops would need more days off in their patterns - ACPO came out against 12 hours for this reason. It would mean individual shift patterns per cop; it would mean accounting for on duty travel time, enhanced airwaves radio coverage, increased 10% payments as even on late shifts officers would be 'on duty' for longer.

This, all of this, shows no concept of operational reality, a smoke and mirrors idea to trick the public into believing more cops are about; when, in truth, the good old Home Sec has just green lighted a reduction in officers at peak policing times. For what? Sadly, it just comes down to money. This is just one reason why the Home Office, the think tanks and the appointed reformers need what some would call a "slapslap". (*A term used to describe a public and quite cheeky telling off*).

Of course, if you introduce a whole range of other measures all of this would go away. Thankfully this hasn't been thought of...oh yeah, it has: Winsor Part 2. This is a sad state of affairs and exactly what should be expected from that big idea factory in the sky. They must not be allowed to dress financial tomfoolery up as police reform. They all need to be "slapslapped" right back to the drawing board and this process needs to begin all over again. Except, this time; leave it to the brave ones on the street, who really know what needs fixing.

The Last Stand:

"This is not a question of causing disaffection or disgrace. We, the sworn few, love this service; we have affection that is unmeasurable"

8th of May 2012

I never thought that The Last Call To Attention
would strike such a chord but, it has. So now
we, together; must take one final stand.

Resignation. Meaning, amongst other things:
the unresisting, acceptance of something as
inescapable; submission. To accept and put up
with. To resign oneself to the inevitable; to
make the best of an undesirable situation. Many
officers feel this, resigned, unresisting, glumly
acceptant. Powerlessly apathetic as the situation
around them spirals ever further out of all
perceived control. We must shake off this
apathy.

To like it or lump it; a phrase usually heard in
situations where no actual choice exists. We
have a choice. We have always had it. Some
officers however feel so acceptant of the fate of
the service, so resigned, that they will do just
that. Resign. Meaning, amongst other things: to
give up a position by formal notification or, to
quit one's office. We cannot give up. We will
not give up our office, the Office of Constable,
so easily.

It has been said that: acceptance has nothing to
do with resignation; it does not mean running
away from the struggle. We must accept that

times are hard, our choices stark; but we must not run. It has been said that: every step toward the goal of justice requires sacrifice, suffering and struggle; the tireless exertions and passionate concern of dedicated individuals. We are those individuals, our families are those individuals. The public are those individuals. We must keep taking those steps.

It has been said that: the probability that we may fail in the struggle ought not to deter us from the support of a cause we believe to be just. Our cause is just and, although now it may seem futile; we will not fail. We do not face simple questions; should we or shouldn't have industrial rights. We would not use them in any case. We should not focus solely on narrow aspects of financial reward and workforce policy; negotiating on a sentence by sentence basis. What we face is much, much deeper, in many ways a much better topic; equally, in many ways, much more difficult. Much worse. An absolutely unique combination.

We must be distracted no more, by the tremors around the police service; the constant external distractions that keep us from the point - that keep subjects just on the tip of our tongue. We must turn our attention inwards; stare coldly at ourselves. This is not a question of causing disaffection or disgrace. We, the sworn few, love this service; we have affection that is unmeasurable. This is about, finally, dealing with the problems in the service, those that are already openly reported and discussed. This is about taking our police service and, by real reform, making it great once more.

The public demand one thing from us, honesty. We must now demand it from ourselves. Being honest can be painful but, even that pain does not cause disaffection; it causes individuals to admit faults. Any pain comes only from dented pride. We are not too far gone; pride is no barrier worth maintaining. We must be brave, bold and direct; we must face our demons head on. If we do not and if we do not do this now… a final resignation for us all.

We must not be subtle or clever. It no longer serves and falls only on the deaf and disbelieving ears of government. We have gone well past persuade, advise and warn. We must use Churchill's pile driver. We must hit the point once, then come back and hit it again. Then hit it a third time - a tremendous whack.

One. Our system is broken.

The target culture forced upon us has gone far

from being a simple measure of Peel's absence of crime. So far in fact, that preventing and detecting crime is often secondary. Secondary to the ongoing manipulation of the number of offences recorded, the type of offence recorded; sanctioned an non-sanctioned finalisations. Squads and squads and squads.

If you ask a Police Constable with twenty-five years service, this was not always the case; once we were all one team. With no agenda other than preventing all crime and catching all criminals. A Constable with this level of service will tell you that the remit culture began to creep in with 'evidence' based promotion. When merit based promotion was declared unsuitable; because it fell out of fashion. Became abused. These constables, our physical memory, see the warning signs and will tell you that we have reached the point of abuse once more. They recognise it but, soon, they will go and our memory will be lost. Their warning, their knowledge, replaced by deafening silence.

We are all Police Officers. Not Neighbourhood Officers, Not Response Officers, Not Squad Officers. Just, sworn holders of the Office of Constable. No division, the same obligations; on duty and off. We are all Police Officers and we do ourselves and the public disservice by eroding our unity.

Senior officers can be found in the media, practically begging for the Home Office to change the rules on recording as it is making crime look ten per cent worse; "It skews figures". The Home Office reply: the rules reflect the law. You are a senior police officer, asking for the rules to be changed as it makes the figures, your figures, look bad. By reflection, you look bad; your pride, ego, dented. These are not mortal wounds or real dangers; get a grip of yourself.

If that is our concern, that we look bad, then we have utterly missed the point of our role; of the duties of our office. I suspect that this plea comes from the fact that it simply impacts upon the ability to 'reflect success' in the evidence-gathering, promotion process; to show some statistical result.

This is massage of statistics and not the absence of crime. It simply allows problems to become established patterns. If it was me I'd have quietly gone about the business of catching the suspects and stopping the commission of offences; then called the press. But then, I am a Police Officer. The target culture has now become engrained and, if you leave something festering for long enough, it will become self-serving, it will become diseased.

Targets, remits; our system is broken because of this and this must be reformed.

Two. Our culture is broken.

Any ex-military personnel who come to the police, to continue to serve their country with discipline, will tell you something clearly. They have years of unblemished service under fire, without issue; they make the transfer and work happily as a Constable, without complaint from the public. This does not concern them; other police officers do.

They will tell you there is a type. A type so alien that their very existence is a complete shock. I can't define it. But, much as I can spot something suspicious in the dead of night, I can see these people clearly, even amongst the crowd. Challenge them, make them feel jealous or inadequate, by doing your job, and they will plunge the knives in your back, just as soon as you turn it. The system of legitimate challenge to inappropriate conduct has been corrupted; become a method of self serving attack.

When we challenge something truly wrong, without agenda, just because it is right; they will attack, heavy and hard. This is their only defence as they cannot understand why someone would do anything, without first planning what box to tick or; how it will give some self-serving advantage. We all see them, have all heard about them, but it has become accepted that, rather than deal with them, reform them, educate them or oust them; we avoid them. In case those knives should head our way the next time our back is turned.

Collective fear of these people by peers, by leaders; has brought us to accept their existence. Allowed us to develop a place for them within the police; where truly there is no place for the self. We feed these people by shuffling them away from us, rather than confronting them. We feed them with evidence gathering, we feed them with remits. We feed these people, we feed our own fear, we feed their agenda; we feed the generational failures that inevitably follow. These people are unmanageable; they will never put themselves second. There is no room for them in our service. We must not fear them and not be scared to admit that they exist. We are running scared in our own house. We stand together in riots, but not in our own stations.

Because of fear, because of ineptitude, because of the system; our culture is broken and must be reformed.

Three. Our leadership is broken.

Broken because of the lure of politics; the culture of smoke and mirrors. Favour and grace. The media have been courted and hospitality taken; then we alienate them almost entirely, spurn them. All because people have been caught out. We restrict contact further because of elections, because we don't want to be seen to take a side; by not talking about real issues that could be twisted and used. In truth, no-one wants to say anything that may be remembered as for or against any potential new 'boss'. This is a nonsense, elections are a sprint; policing is the infinite marathon. Unfortunately, politics in policing is alive and well; being encouraged by exactly this kind of behaviour.

The lure of the private sector, post retirement, after years of experience in an evidence based promotion system; drives relentless change. Sometimes it has been based on previous experience, with little or no time to fully examine the key differences in the challenges faced. All for what, an address book that has monetary value?

Our selection process, evidence based promotion has become corrupted; and the future of this is self perpetuating. Policy has been designed that prohibits best candidate; replacing it with a positive action policy. Equality means, quite simply, that everyone has a level playing field. I say that to cause no stir, but because it is true; and always has been. Police Officers, real coppers, spend every day levelling the playing field for those that cannot do it themselves. We need to look much more deeply at what is causing issues of 'representation' within the rank structure; what are the real barriers?

Our leadership, the last 'coppers' up at the dizzying heights, must see that underneath them, heading towards them; is a generation of flawed culture, flawed system product. They must see it and they must feel it is now too late to stop it. Police Officers, with rare exceptions, do not look or sound like those cast in this mould at all. We are the public and they are us. Police Officers do not speak in nonsense riddles; increasingly one of the greatest reasons we are not trusted is because we sound further from the public daily.

They, the last coppers at the top, must be terrified as they have, effectively, let it happen. Stoked some of the fires even. This 'new' leadership will mould in its own image, recruit in its own image and, as we breed this culture, as direct entry fans the flames; who will do the front line policing? Who will get their hands dirty while these people are out to gather evidence and statistics? Probably, a subsidiary of, a supermarket chain. People have clearly seen this coming and privatisation is the only logical response, the only way to stop the police becoming this; to kill a monster that bears their name.

Because of politics, because of post-career opportunities and address books, because of evidence gathering, because of fear, because of moulding, because Police Officers are frowned upon; because our culture is broken, because our system is broken: our leadership is broken and must be reformed.

Because of all of this, because we have not dealt with this; the reforms that come are not operational, not practical. Simply put, they are fiscal and driven by agenda; driven by quiet whispers in friendly ears.

Our system, culture and leadership is broken; a self perpetuating vicious circle that keeps us broken. Our reform is, by default, broken. This is our tremendous whack.

The Police Service, as a whole, is broken and that is what needs to be reformed. Until that is done and the dust has begun to settle, no financial attack on our livelihoods is permissible, acceptable or just. Real savings come from fixing what is broken, from stopping the rot and going back, completely back, to basics; no agenda other than fighting crime. No squads, no easy rides, no fear. Real police work. A reinforced thin blue line, out on the street, preventing crime because we promised to. Salaries, pensions, redundancies; all a tiny fragment of the true savings to be had. Winsor in truth is just another deflection from the real issues. More smoke, more mirrors.

Within our ranks there is no space for the bigoted, ineffective, the corrupt; not in any of their many disguises. I said this and I meant it. We see first hand the effects of agenda, half truth and blatant, statistical manipulation. I see it, you see it. We all are touched by it.

The biggest threat to us has always been self interest. Nothing changes; until we change it.

Until we stop being scared in our own house. United we stand, behind the oaths that bind us. Some of us, without agenda, fear or affection, malice or ill-will; the sworn few.

If we, Police Officers, want to make this change we must do so now. It will neither be easy, nor pleasant; but we have dealt with much worse in our careers. The things that will stay with us, haunt us forever. We can do this but, we must do so with the full consent and support of the public; without this we can do nothing. The future of British policing lies in their hands. So, to the public:

Ask yourselves, what do you want from your police service? Fearless honesty, crime fighting without agenda; or, are you also resigned to the situation that exists, to what will almost inevitably follow? We lay the choice rightly with you, your decision and, although we may have forgotten for a time; it always has been yours to make. We are you and, without you, we are nothing; we resign by default.

The sworn few stand to attention, having been called; we stand with you, we stand for you. We stand together. We ask you, can you, will you, stand with us; this last time? If you want Police Officers, the sworn few, to fix this service, reform it, make it what it should be; if that is what you decide. Then shout loud, shout long and shout hard. Make your voices heard above all other noise.

We are here, your Police Officers, we are waiting and, when you call…if you call; we will be there, ready to do what needs to be done.

The End of The Beginning:

"People need to know us as individuals, know what
we stand for. Know that we mean it"

15th of May 2012

For me thoughts frequently come back to
Winston Churchill. He was a man with huge
issues, massive flaws. He was human; and that
is why I hold him in such high regard. He
embraced his problems and they did not prevent
him from taking one of the greatest stands in
recent history. He was witty at a time of
catastrophe, he was to the point, often abrupt;
he did something great. He united and inspired,
not just one nation but many, to overcome
adversity. To quote the man himself, in a way
that is relevant to what must come next:

"Now this is not the end. It is not even the
beginning of the end. But it is, perhaps, the end
of the beginning".

When I wrote the *Last the Call to Attention*, it
wasn't because I genuinely thought the end of
the Police, an absolute finish, was coming. I did
it because I wanted to offer a very public
reminder about something that had never really
gone away; our sense of duty, our morality, the
fact that we are bound by our oaths and still
stand, as the sworn few, no matter what is
happening in the world around us. We hold the
line. We are the calm before, during and after
the storm. We needed that call and, it seemed,
the message wasn't going to be forthcoming
from above.

When I wrote The Last Stand, it wasn't because I thought Rome was falling and figured it would be best to pick up a sledgehammer and take it to the service, rather than leave someone else to do it. I wrote it because I wanted us to face up, to really face up, to some of the problems that exist that we continue to tip-toe around; for fear of punishment, or fear that we will allow those who have us in their sights to load more ammunition. No fear. No affection. That applies even to ourselves. We are the last guardians of morality and with that comes the responsibility for our own domain.

Far from being the end, those two pieces were the beginning of something. However, unlike the Police, beginnings do have an end. What I have come to realise is that there are good cops out there, an overwhelming majority. We do believe in our oaths, we do want the service to be better; each of us cares about the public.

I have come to realise that the general public do support us, do want the good cops out there. They believe, having seen us speaking openly and candidly, that we believe in our oaths, that we want the service to better; that each of us cares about them. I have also come to realise though, that there are still so many issues of trust, so many engrained illusions and delusions that it will be difficult for all people to understand us without more work; without our stall being laid out more clearly, more publicly. More openly.

People need to know us as individuals, know what we stand for. Know that we mean it. That is the only way we can ever fully overcome the police/public divide. It has to start somewhere, it has to start with someone; someone has to be the first to tread the path otherwise no-one will ever find out where it leads...

My name is James. I'm 32. (My birthday is within days but I'm ignoring that for as long as possible). I am a husband and haven't always been the best at it. I am a father and will be the best at that if it kills me. My first home was a council house, my family is now utterly dysfunctional, the centre ripped out of it when my mum died way back in 2001. But, before that, I was brought up with good values, humour, decency, honesty (even when the truth hurts) and respect for the values and opinions of others; even when you disagree with them.

I found school too easy and not a source of enough stimulation to harness my concentration, so, I coasted out of it with GCSE's and went to work at seventeen. Until

2004 I just did whatever I needed to do, to pay the bills. (When I say whatever I mean it, I've been from Mortgage Advisor to IT and, at one point, was hauling boxes at the airport from 2am until 6am then putting in a twelve hour day, doing back-breaking Grounds Maintenance).

I joined the Police on the 10th of May 2004 and have never looked back. I found myself in a promise made, in front of a packed room of strangers.

I say on monitoring forms that I am a Christian and, believe me, there have been days when I have talked at length to God, but I don't go to church. As far as I am aware I am one of the only 'Lapsed Christian' Police Officers to have driven around, daily, in a bright red, 1969 Pontiac Firebird, blasting out *N.W.A*.

I am a fully qualified Sergeant but can't pass through the promotion system to gain my stripes, I just don't understand how it works. Still, I have been carrying out the role of Sergeant, either Temporary or Acting since 2008.

I have been commended four times, for closing a whole block of flats as a crack house, for bravery at a fatal care home fire, for the arrest of a very dangerous individual armed with a knife who had attacked two members of the public, unprovoked; for leadership. I get personal thank you letters from ranking officers for arresting rapists, burglars, paedophiles. In all of this I get a little bit uncomfortable, I just see it as doing my job. No-one has ever ordered me to do any of these things; I do them because that is what I am there to do; much as it was once to make sure a lawn was perfectly striped at a Wedding Venue. Also to consider is the horror of the 'ceremony photograph'; I pull the most amazing faces when someone first advises me that a photo MUST be taken. You should see my warrant card.

I've stood in front of neighbourhood forums in the worst areas of my force and turned stony, disbelief in words spoken, into standing ovations for actions taken. I did this, not by magic, but by doing my job and being honest about what I could and would do; I never break my promises, I will always find a way. (On the rare occasions were I can't find a way, I'll say so and explain why).

I derive more comfortable pleasure, from the little thank you notes I've been passed; my favourite being from a lady who's bike I rescued. I think it is was Einstein who said there is no such thing as a big or small problem. There are just problems and my job is to resolve them, that's what I promised, to protect and to serve. I never saw any clause that said I must be selective about it and, I think, this is exactly how the wider public see it too.

I carry a lot of weight on my shoulders, things that other people should not have to know, I have cut cable ties from where they should never have been in the first place. I do not talk about this with my family or anyone who asks because it is not for them; there are some things that nobody needs to know.

I am not scared of anyone; if I think something is wrong I will do all that I can to set it right, and even when I finally hit a wall, I may still be inclined to repeatedly bang against it to see if there is any give in the mortar lines. I will do this beyond the point where it hurts me. Equally, If I think something is right, or there is a better way of doing things, I will knock on doors until one is opened and someone listens. People who know me, know this. I will not back down, never give up, never surrender.

I know my job, inside out and, what I don't know, I know how to find it out and quickly. I make it my business to know. If I see people who are not doing their job properly or acting in a questionable way, I will take action, no matter what the personal consequences.

I have, do and will continue to tell people things they might not want to hear; that is part and parcel of what I do. It doesn't matter to me who that person is, where they come from or what they represent. I won't apologise for this but I can guarantee you that it is never for any reason, other than I am doing what is required of me.

When I make an error or mistake, I will admit it and rectify it, immediately. Policing is never personal. No malice, no ill-will.

I have, do and will continue to help people, indiscriminately, when they need to be helped; that is also part and parcel of what I do. I will not conform to quotas, never have and never will; they are wholly inappropriate, in my opinion, in the context of the police; but if I am managing a person and see they produce absolutely nothing, the reasons will be looked at and the issues will be dealt with.

I will always take part in a productive debate or discussion but, that is reliant on the ability of the other person to sit down and listen as well as stand up and shout. Sometimes, just sometimes I may have to play a legal trump card, but not without having a reason and explaining it first; and when I do take that step, all I ask is that people listen to what I'm saying. It makes the experience more positive and genuine. It stops the proliferation of animosity and fosters better understanding for the future. Confrontation is not a desirable result for anyone.

So, this is me. James. Just a normal bloke, a hard working fella.

What I hope you know now is that, although I am not perfect - far from it - I am dedicated, tenacious and will put myself second, third or even fourth; to make sure that I am doing the right thing by you. I am a good bobby, a decent cop. What I hope you know now is that, I will do whatever needs to be done, to protect you, to serve you in the capacity of my office. I will take on giants without fear and am not so blinded by affection that I won't deal with problems within the service.

This is the end of the beginning, the cards are on the table, you know that people are out there, people like me. People who are just like

you; who just happen to wear a uniform.
I make no judgements, so pass none on me,
until of course, you know me; after that you can
think whatever you like and I will respect your
opinion. Although, as previously stated, I may
not agree with it. I hope this has gone some
way to creating a fresh start, for all of us. The
much needed new beginning that will allow us
to reconcile the differences that have grown,
bridge the gap between us; Police and public. I
am not against you, I am for you. I will do
whatever needs to be done, nothing to big or
small, in order to keep my promise (I don't
break them). Above all, you now know that I
am not alone.

I started this with Winston Churchill and it
seems fitting that the end of the beginning
should conclude in the same way.
    "All the great things are simple, and many
can be expressed in a single word; freedom,
justice, honour, duty, mercy, hope". I want to
open a new chapter here so I must make sure I
set the right tone; I must get this right. So, I'm
going to keep it simple and hopefully great, as
can be. My promise to you, is this: I will
protect and serve.

The Boys are Back in Town:

"It is very easy to take a perceived victory, in one small battle, as a sign that the war is won"

17th of May 2012

I've been watching closely, the last few weeks, seeing how the police fight back against the proposed reforms develops. It will directly affect me, my family and yet I feel almost completely alien to it. Like it's happening in the main in a far away place, where the echo takes time to filter down to us mortals.

This is not through lack of knowledge of the topic, talk about Winsor and I can tell you've I've even read the minutes, of the individual consultations. Talk about media coverage, I have them all on multi link feeds. Talk about politics, finance, big business and policy, I've unpicked that thread and I wish I hadn't. I just find that watching all of this unfold through the official channels, on all sides, is like watching a TV in a vat of treacle. Weird, one way and hard to get any real sense of.

Tonight I made a post on twitter, it read:
   "A man can't be too careful in the choice of his enemies.

Federation for his forty minute speech and his 'hands up' gag.

I saw the quiet dignity of the 10th of May march replaced by House of Commons level heckles, which even we weren't comfortable with. I saw a political side being nodded to; I saw applause for Labour, when only years ago we derided them eroding our office with PCSOs. I saw Ms May looking uncomfortable, upset and angry. I saw people shouting victory.

It is very easy to take a perceived victory, in one small battle, as a sign that the war is won and I can't blame people for the strut that followed the Home Secretary's appearance, there's a lot of frustration pent up beyond breaking point. I could almost here *Thin Lizzy* as the soundtrack to what is being talked about.

My dear old Nan,who taught me never to feed hungry crocodiles, also taught me that 'Hell hath no fury like a woman scorned'. Ms May is not only a woman but a politician, who wields significant power over our futures, the heckling was scorn, heaped on and, worse; it was made to feel personal.

You might disagree with some or all of this but, the facts is, we all promise no fear or affection, no malice or ill-will. We are better than that type of scorn, it undermines us and if we genuinely are to stand any chance in making this true reform, for the better, then we must not fall into such traps. We must keep the fight on the high ground or, risk losing altogether.

We lost ground, we played to the image of a bunch of union members making noise for money; we don't even have a union because we cannot have one; yet that image is very hard to shake off. The old proverb is true, it sticks. Any PR savvy government officer would know this and we walked straight into it; almost ran. We can expect the fury and we can expect it along these lines. And, where once we could have relied upon certain press outlets, look at what's happening, look at Leveson; look at phone hacking.

There is no action without consequence and when the press do not leap to take our side, we should not be surprised or turn our heckles on them.

I watched that night, after Ms May appeared and, on Channel 4 News and I saw it, clear as day. I saw the trumpeted triumph of earlier further disarmed in one sentence, in words to the effect of:

"We agree, the police do deserve better".

My dear old Nan taught me something else you see, relevant here and a portent, if you like, of the second strategy that will be used against us. There is no better revenge than open sympathy or forgiveness. There is no sufficient counter argument to someone who appears to agree with you or publicly pats you on the back and says 'there-there'.

This has been planned over a long period of time. I make no bones about it. If we are fighting for ourselves then we should wave the flag now and take what comes. If however, we are fighting for something more than ourselves; for the police, for the office of constable, for the good of the public: then we have some growing up to do and, we have to do it fast. We need to reach into the issues that face us every day, for therein lies the way in which we will take back the ground we lost and, maybe, win more than the battle. Think about it, when people see the police, they no longer think 'hero'; they see a pantomime villain. This was not always the case and we need to be asking ourselves, why?

We have been constantly beaten, smashed onto the rocks by the vast array of competing and constantly changing demands placed upon us; knocked into the ropes, blow after blow, to the point where we are now. We are seen as the street-level face of the power, heartless agents of government; because we have been put there. We are often the only contact people have with authority and as such we are easy to hate, hard to love; the urge to fight us is overwhelming and it shows on many fronts. Politically slanted drive and corporate, financial agenda, work hand-in-hand, always cascading down to us; and it is here, between us and the public that the street level confrontation lies. Those in the corridors of power and financial influence do not want this kind of kerfuffle on their doorstep; they have been only too happy to create and maintain a system, that keeps the dirt off their shoes and the blood off their hands.

Our only weapon is going to be the ability to bridge the divide, remove the wedge driven between the police and public . By doing that, the influence of politics and money can be driven out forever. We are a service for the people, made up of the people we are sworn to serve and protect. We need to be reminded, to remind ourselves and everyone else, that we are there for the public and equally, that same public must still want us to do it; impartially, without other agenda than truth and justice. If we can reconnect with the public on the street, then we can shake the establishment, to the foundations. That has to be our way forwards. United we must stand. For us that means no more heckling, no more letting it get personal; no more playing into stereotypes of boisterous, union boys.

We have made good ground, because of the tireless efforts and dedicated individuals who have started to inspire renewed public support; take one look at the #Antiwinsornetwork. However, we have much more to do. If we don't do it then we must accept that we've not been wise in the making of our enemies. If we do, if we rise above the nonsense and show ourselves for what we are; selfless, honest, normal people, keeping their promises. If we can show everyone, without exception, what the police should be, what police officers are, what we were originally meant for and why we are here; why we are still needed. If we can go back to the very start and be heroes and heroines to ALL people once again...If we can do that; then we may be justified, as we go about our daily business, if we are quietly singing:

"Spread the word around. Guess who's back in town. You spread the word around".

The Police Reform Show

Part 1:

"it wasn't exactly the rumble in the jungle it was
more of a whisper in the trees"

20th of May 2012

12.20 on Sunday the 20th of May saw Police Reform make a foray into the Sunday Politics Show on the BBC. In the weekly 'Head to Head' section, Police Federation Chairman Paul McKeever and Crime and Justice Minister Nick Herbert faced each other across the table.

The Chair, Andrew Neil, from the outset looked marginally unimpressed with either side of the argument; If anything he showed a form of mild amusement, at the end of the allowed time saying; "they're still going". And, herein lies the issue; it wasn't exactly 'the rumble in the jungle' it was more of a 'whisper in the trees'.

McKeever stuck to his line, concern over the impact on the wider public,rather than pay but was subjected to an uncomfortable camera pan out, around the time that fitness was mentioned. Herbert on the other hand, appeared mildly annoyed throughout; a constant undertone of a person who sees themselves as dealing with an idiot, who just won't listen. There were tickles of the real issues, those that need to be in the foreground but there was no boom-bash-crash of those issues being launched into the audience-sphere, to bring the police reform issue to the forefront of public consciousness. Head to Head began with a short introduction piece by Giles Dilnot, opening with the line that the government see the police as the last unreformed public service, the last major change being around thirty years ago. The Home Secretary was shown saying that the police must take their part of public sector pain and that there are roles which civilians could do, more cheaply.

The appointed man in charge of the Independent Review, Tom Winsor was shown, stating that the whole reform was geared towards an effective pay rise for those working in the front line, those in the wet and cold facing 'the angry man'. He made clear his view that the reform was not political or ideological.

Dilnot stated that many police officers agree that reform is needed, something we all know, but made a point of stating that it was privatisation making officers feel the most uneasy. He stated that many of us worry about the job getting more out of us, than we do out of it.

There was a brief mention of the reforms of 1993, largely abandoned by Michael Howard when David Cameron was his assistant. The so called 'Sheehy Report' was very, very similar to Winsor and carried, for the most part, many of the same counter arguments from the Federation. The report proposed reduction in starting wages, performance related pay, fixed term commissions.

With Dilnot's introduction over, the Head to Head began with McKeever; the police were the first service to call for a Royal Commission, the police had listened to Her Majesty's Inspectorate of Constabulary and accepted a figure of 12% as an achievable level of cuts. Herbert was quick to reply that the Police, as a whole, is opposed generically to all reform and cited resistance to PCSOs when they were first introduced and even traffic wardens. The retort was clearly designed to paint a picture of a group resistant to change but was largely undermined by McKeever's opening.

McKeever replied with acceptance of reforms to pensions but weakened the argument with the addition of 'we have no rights to contest it in any case' disclaimer. He then moved on swiftly to sating that Winsor opened the door to privatisation but kept the reason why unmentioned. He then moved on a again to the magic figure of 16,000 officers expected to be cut being the same level of officers it took to quell the London Riots 2011. These are both potent arguments that came across as bullet points, losing their immediate power and impact in the process.

Herbert seized on this and denied privatisation having anything to do with Winsor then leapt straight onto the increase in fitness levels the Winsor reforms would bring. This is a populist argument that feeds the international doughnut shop anecdote. It is a low blow but consistently effective. Herbert then moved straight into the facts and figures on the numbers of officers in restricted duties, back office posts; again this is a populist but weighty argument that has captured the imagination of the media throughout this process.

McKeever's come back was weaker this time; a dismissive but strangely quiet 'we're negotiating on fitness'. The follow up was the stronger argument about the erosion of the office of constable, which the public understand and hold dear. This again was bullet pointed and had numerous for and against arguments which made it unwise to use in such a short form.

Herbert was quick on this; "you can't keep using that argument Paul" and "the claims just don't stand up". McKeever replied to privatisation again, citing the West Midlands/Surrey tendering process as including public patrols in the detail. Herbert's retort, we wouldn't give them the powers to do that piece of it anyway. McKeever spoke of fairness to officers, of a 25-30% loss in personal spending power. Herbert came straight back, a little too quickly this time, Winsor doesn't change the system. For the first time Neil interjected, asking McKeever direct, "Do the police still have the best pension and pay in the public sector?". This is the biggest argument gun Herbert had and the trigger was pulled for him. McKeever could only come back by saying yes. This is a substantial weakening of all the 'police-side' arguments put forward. Even trying to pursue the question with his 'astonishment at the low priority given to the police by the government' and that 'the police were picking up the pieces for other parts of the public sector, like Social Services'; after the landing of the big artillery round it was all but lost.

Herbert was on this again, making clear that cops still have a deal which puts them 15% better off than other public sector workers, driving a wedge that is more like an open wound. Neil came back in then, giving Herbert a taste; this time pointing out that officer numbers were already down by thousands, from 143 to 135,000. Herbert resorted to pointing out that 6,000 officers of those left were on restricted duties in any case.

McKeever delivered a good finish, highlighting the government had increased International AID by 34%, more than the total spend on British Policing. Herbert's finish was weaker; "there is not a force in the country that is facing a 20% cut".

Overall, McKeever nil, Herbert Nil. Andrew Neil, 2.

The Police Reform Show

Part 2:

"Until we understand it, until we talk about it, we can't effectively relate to the public about what is happening"

Sunday 20th May 2012

I sincerely hope that by now, at least those of you who have read me before, would know that Part 1 of this blog was very out of character. It was neutral, almost devoid of any passion for the office that I hold. It was unusual but, not without purpose. This is lengthy, involves some active participation from you and, in case you were having doubts; stick with it, this is me remember. My apology up front is that this is not my usual, literary standard but: I am only human.

With Part 1, I wanted to show how both sides of the argument look to someone who has no emotional involvement or, clear understanding of policing or, indeed, the true meaning of the reforms that are being negotiated. I wanted to show how fundamentally disengaging the debate is. I wanted us, all of us, to be able to see this through the eyes of the wider public; as it is being represented by the less sensational representatives of the media.

We all know that any debate is only won, when an independent party chooses a side; that party is the currently disengaged, wider public. My point about the only way forwards being in the full engagement of the public; about winning the battle of hearts and minds, if you want to see it that way, is now largely made out. Only those of us who already know about each of the issues, in depth, has had anything to say about today's Politics Show; or worse, has shown any more than a trifling interest.

We must change this and the power lies only within us. We have much work to do. We are hard to love, us cops. We also know that we are fighting a long term battle. So, the first thing we need to do is think about strategy; what is it? Or, more importantly; what could it be? Let's begin by hypothesising; an important tack to take, as hypothesis is just free and harmless thought. Let's imagine, because this is imaginary, that your ultimate goal is to introduce the free market into aspects of the public sector where it previously has had little, or limited, access.

Firstly, you would have to have an ideal outcome, say the privatisation of something, but you know that your goal would not go down well. What would you do? Well, you would have to firstly set it up, without saying that was what you were doing. Something independent would be a good place to begin, especially if it recommended a series of items for implementation that would facilitate your goal but, crucially, not shout about it. You would have to know that this had been objected to before and, you would have to count on the objections being largely similar; so you could account for them in your wider strategy.

On top of this you would need a media campaign, chipping away at faults with what you were trying to 'free market' and, on top of that again, you would need to ensure that some sort of non biased organisation was supporting your side of the argument. To make your side of the debate appear more persuasive.

Lastly, you would desire two further things; One, you would want any confrontation over the issue to be as understated, as forgettable, as possible and also reflect poorly, if achievable, on those resisting you. Two, you would want to bury it behind some sort of mass media, global event; to ensure that when it went ahead, directly afterwards, any final objections were buried and the whole thing happened very quietly.

Of course, you should always have a trump card up your sleeve and if there was some way, at that global event, that you could successfully showcase the exact types of privatisation that were part of your goal; then wouldn't that be perfect? But this is, of course, all just hypothesis, a little bit of harmless imagination, just to blow out some cobwebs.

Now, back to the points from the Sunday Politics show, a very understated confrontation if ever I saw one; especially following the wide furore of disapproval, caused by the Federation booing the Home Secretary. I must make clear, all I am doing here on in, is raising things of potential interest, which are readily available on the internet and; applying them to the context of items raised within the show. My only intention is that you look at what is out there, further research it, if you see fit or, alternatively; just discuss and debate it.

Discussion and debate is one of the healthiest things in our society and, if it is informed; it can only bring about a healthier state of things.

The first point to be raised is the Independent Review, conducted by Tom Winsor; in his words definitely 'not political or ideological'.

Well, we could personally attack Tom Winsor, or his recommendations; but why? He wrote a report of incredible detail, based on extensive consultation, on a topic of which he is no expert. He is in fact a former Rail Regulator and a partner at law firm White an Case. A firm who recently represented G4S in the preparation of their contract, for service provision with Lincolnshire Police, to the tune of £200 Million. (**1**). This is no secret though, it was brought up at the Federation conference last week and reported by the BBC (**2**).

He relied on the input of all of us to draw his conclusions, and sometimes we just didn't turn up. Look no further than the seminar transcripts: (Page 3, Line 3-6 on Basic Pay as one example...**3**). He relied on the experts assigned to assist and, he acknowledges this in the opening pages of Winsor Part 2. (Page 8...**4**)

One of those expert advisers, Sir Edward Crew QPM was a former chief of police, so clearly brought a balanced view of all aspects of the profession (and each side involved) with him. A quick search engine entry of his name will bring you an article from 2001 in which he had some staff issues and a slight problem with the Federation (**5**).

Keep searching and you will find him listed as the Patron of the Security Export Focus Group (SEFG), at ADS, the trade organisation advancing the UK Aerospace, Defence, Security and Space industries.

ADS was formed from the merger of the Association of Police and Public Security Suppliers (APPSS), the Defence Manufacturers Association (DMA) and the Society of British Aerospace Companies (SBAC) in October 2009. Together with its regional partners, ADS represents over 2,600 companies. (**6**).

Further searches find a further listing, for Sir Edward, as a member of the executive team at: Team Assure (**7**). The website of Team Assure states "Assure consultants are recognised by their peers as leaders in their sector of security, risk and resilience". He certainly keeps himself in the loop.

Of course, beyond all of this extra reading, it is worth reading the 1993 Sheehy Report on Police Pay and Conditions, which recommended, amongst other things, a reduction in basic salary, performance related pay, fixed term commissions for police officers. It is markedly similar in many ways to Winsor's recommendations and also, so I'm told, a speech made by Prime Minister David Cameron, in 2006. I haven't seen this myself but keep meaning to get to it. At the time Michael Howard, who had just replaced Ken Clarke didn't take up Sheehy. But he did have Mr Cameron as his assistant on the matter.

Moving on, Winsor was mentioned as potentially opening the door to privatisation but, this was not elaborated upon. Perhaps it should have been; does it open that door?

Well, maybe, but it depends on how you read this article. Lord Blair was recently featured in The Guardian on the 4th March 2012 (**8**) and in it he talks exclusively about privatisation, making this statement at the beginning of the article:

"The first, a mistake in the face of looming cuts – 20%, more than almost any other service – was to ask Her Majesty's Inspectorate of Constabulary to determine which police officer jobs could be classified as back- and middle-office tasks so as to protect front-line services. That rather pointless inquiry, which inevitably found most of the jobs could not be separated by that terminology, has delayed the impact of the second and much more important decision: that the political shibboleth of officer numbers would be abandoned and police numbers would be allowed to fall. That is what lies behind the tenders put out by West Midlands and Surrey police forces, central to the claim that the police are being privatised."

He goes on to say:

"Once the straitjacket of officer numbers is

removed, police forces can modernise their budgets in the way any other institution would do, namely by reducing unit costs."

One of the most important recommendations of the Winsor Report is compulsory redundancy. That would be helpful in such a scenario, wouldn't it? It is of course interesting to note that privatisation plans mentioned in this article have caused quite a lot of concern and the last trace I find, is of them being put on hold (**9**). This is far from the end of what you can find, when you have a quick look for what is openly out there. For now, however, I have a shirt to iron and an alarm clock to set. These are just some of the voids that we must fill in, so that each of us understands and discusses, in full, what we are going through as a service. Until we understand it, until we talk about it, we can't effectively relate to the public about what is happening. If I could give you one piece of advice, if you would still take it; get reading, start talking.

I hope, before bed, that this has been informative and will be a source of discussion and debate. I also hope, that if you thought badly of me for writing Part 1, that I am in some way forgiven.

The Anti Winsor Report 1 & 2:

"The immediate initiation of a full inquiry into policing and police reform"

31ˢᵗ of May 2012

This forty page, two part, research report was posted by Occupy Police on their website: *www.occupypolice.org*

I am not including the reports here; they make lengthy and uncomfortable reading but, really galvanised me to keep raising my game, to take a much deeper look at what I was blogging about. I would highly recommend, that when you have finished reading this book that you get on the internet, get a stiff drink and read what you find (**10**).

The report makes ten recommendations, none of which I, nor any sane person I have spoken to, disagrees with. They are, therefore, something that is worth reproducing here without the need to look elsewhere, in particular as they have been ignored since their publication at the end of May and, as I have referenced the report itself (and the recommendations) in subsequent blogs and open emails.

If you've never seen these before, I think you, like many others, may be looking up that link at lot quicker than you might have thought.

1) The immediate initiation of a full inquiry into policing and police reform and until such time as the below inquiry topics have been resolved, the current police reforms, including those relating to Winsor Part 2 are to be placed on immediate hold.

2)The extent of this private industry link and, the influence this has had on the process and progress of the police service as a whole and, the current reform agenda, must be explored and probed in full.

3) The extent of the links between ex and serving senior officers and, the influence this has had on the process and progress of the current reform agenda, must be explored and probed in full.

4) The link between White Case, the legal firm of Tom Winsor (Independent Police Review Lead) and G4S must be probed and it decided whether there was a potential or apparent conflict of interest, taking into consideration the full reform agenda.

5) The link between ADS and Sir Edward Crew, principle professional assistant of Tom Winsor, must be explored in full as must his activities in his ADS capacity, to ensure that

there has been no potential or actual conflict of interest or cross-over between future business interests and reforms made to the structure and format of the police.

6) The link between think tanks and donations must be fully explored to ascertain whether or not lobbying or business influence on government policy, has taken or is taking place, either deliberately or by coincidence. This incorporates 'sponsored events'.

7) The links betweens individuals holding current public offices and those working within the think tanks must be fully explored to ascertain whether boundaries are being stretched or abused.

8) The link between think tank donations by foreign donors and party donations must be fully explored to establish whether there should be concern about party support by alternative or prohibited methods.

9) The link between think tanks and the media must be explored to preserve the impartiality of the press, by means of ensuring it has not and is not being used to control or influence content.

10) The link between Prof Richard Disney, principle advisor to Tom Winsor, and the LSE / Institute of fiscal studies must be explored to ensure impartiality in his input.

Open Email - Home Affairs Select Committee:

"this is not about pay, conditions, pensions"

7th of June 2012

For The Attention of The Chairman:

Sir,

I make clear from the out-set; this is not about pay, conditions, pensions or bringing the service into disrepute. All except the latter are out of my control in any case. I am a dedicated, serving officer, who loves the police, a service for the public, made up of the public. I want people to be proud of that which I serve in.

Nonetheless, I find myself gravely concerned about the ongoing and escalating reforms; some of which have been passed and some of which are yet to be ratified.

Recent announcements alone are disturbing enough; that the legal firm White and Case was paid direct for Tom Winsor's time, while they were representing G4S in a £200million pound contract with Lincolnshire Police. That Home Secretary, Theresa May, emphatically stated there was no conflict in this. That Tom Winsor has today been announced as the preferred candidate for the head of Her Majesty's Inspectorate, again by the Home Secretary.

There is sufficient, publicly accessible information, to cause further unease, so much so that to grasp it is sickening.

ACPO are effectively running a business and MP Julian Smith has had recent cause to bring their activities, in particular 'consultancy' payments into open question. All the while they have remained silent to their officers on the reform agenda, but sufficient has been said, about the vast numbers of officers to be 'lost' post Olympics, to make most of us that serve feel very worried for the future. Especially when we saw first-hand, only last year, what can happen when there are 'mobilisation' issues.

Many former ACPO rank officers now sit on the boards of some of the large security companies that are poised to bid for 'privatisation' contracts, this is no secret; nor that many of them remain ACPO, lifetime members. The question of concern can only and, quite fairly, be: does this influence decision making? It is not a question I can answer. Nor can I answer whether Sir Edward Crew, principal assistant to Tom Winsor, has any relevant or even conflicting interests, arising from his patronage at ADS or his position at Team Assure. All I knew about him a few weeks ago is that there was a no confidence vote in him, in 2001, when he was the Chief Constable of West Midlands Police.

Beyond ACPO, beyond the service itself I have found that there is a web-like infrastructure of think tanks, each openly linked or in some cases, started by, politicians. Within them and between them a constant movement of staff, for example Blair Gibbs, now head of Crime and Justice at Policy Exchange, having been staff officer for Crime and Justice Minister Nick Herbert (formerly of think tank Reform himself).

As you, no doubt are aware, the Policy Exchange now has a substantial income, some coming from the corporate engagement forum, with notable 'clients' such as BskyB and BUPA to name but a few; not that it has not had it's problems, with Channel 4 Dispatches and the Charity Commission to name but a few. It also seems to have a board made up largely of business men and 'the media'.

It seems to me, as a normal person and as a police officer that there are things about these arrangements which desperately need a public airing; if only to set people's mind at rest. There has been an incredible amount of research put into this, to provide the beginnings of a more rounded picture and this can be found by following this internet link: (**10**). You may be surprised at the source, you may not. In any case the information has been verified via the appendices and some open source research using a widely available search engine.

That report does make recommendations and, from a personal perspective, I would feel much better if I could answer those questions; before this service is 'reformed' beyond all recognition. I cannot however tell you what to do, having seen you in action, I trust your moral compass. I thank you for any time you can spare in digesting this letter.

With respect and the best of intentions.

The Blue Collar Blog:

"My clock-machine is more imaginary than the copper that Policy Exchange idiot saw on a bus"

12th of June 2012

This is a self parody of sorts. If you are easily offended do not read this. You have been warned...

When I left school, at 17, with only GCSEs (because I was bored and frankly more interested in money and minky at weekends): I went to work in a factory. Thorntons to be precise. I was first a fudge-packer then a toffee-smasher before being elevated to the dizzying heights of box-crusher. This means I was 'blue collar'; with a penchant for strawberry creams.

I once gave a girl called Sarah a lift and fingered her, right in the Fiesta; for which she gave a fake, Stone Island jumper. I wore it to watch my mates play football for the town team while drinking warm lager straight from the can; bought with my hard earned chocolate pennies. I shouted rude words at the other team and visually impaired ref. This means I was blue collar.

I once got in a nose to nose with a total arsehole because he tried to crush me with a forklift as a birthday 'joke'. Later he bought me a 12p cup of subsidised tea and sulkily apologised. He's still an arsehole. That means I was blue collar.

Apart from one nasty episode when 'the beast' gorged on diabetic chocolates until she involuntarily shit herself at the production line; nothing particularly unpleasant, nor challenging happened at all. Because at the time I was blue collar. I clocked in and out on time. I went to the pub and most days I was home in time for tea and a frantic, teenage wank.

Note I say I was blue collar and note that I a) had fun being it and b) boldly state it was no bad thing. In fact, I can still quite happily talk like I'm 'blue collar' which has saved my arse from a beating more than thrice. In fact, today, for the first time since the 90's I have actually been called a 'blue collar clock in clock out' worker; so in a departure from my norm; I shall continue to use what I was to relate my feelings as such.

First things first then; when some jumped up moron and his pretentious toffee nosed mates call me names...they ought to have the cojones to front me up and say "I say that" not revert to the tactics of a weeping pussy and dribble on that "someone else thinks that, I'm just saying it". Grow a pair, bell end. Next, how dare you?

Clock in clock out? You cheeky prat. For the last eight years I've worked thousands of hours above and beyond humane treatment because I can't just pack up my toys and fuck off when the whistle blows; and in case you think I'm taking the piss on overtime you can have my payslips. Like many of my colleagues I don't claim it; because we're dedicated crown servants. Or mugs if you prefer.

When you've been awake for 36 hours and are still going I'll let you comment; until then wind your neck in you weasel.
As for blue collar; it's not a fucking sausage factory. Or don't you know? No I forgot; you have no clue. It doesn't go chugga-chugga-choo-choo. Nor as it goes do your god awful nose up, broom up the arse mates; who look at the rest of us with the mild amusement of a sociopathic kids torching ants with a Bunsen burner.

You are fucking with people's live; with safety of men, women and children up and down the country and you moan and sneer like a bunch of spoilt brats when we point it out. Spineless.

Searching a rotting corpse is not blue collar, nor is keeping composure when you deal with the neighbours, family, coroner; and then write a detailed file. All the while the smell of death hanging in the back of your nose as you force down a peperami (because you can hold the pack without touching the food).

Leading the screaming injured teenagers out of the house doused in paraffin then going back in to nick the deranged father; while he tries to burn all of you with thankfully wet matches; is not blue collar. Then the witness interviews with hysterical and confused teens, the debrief, the case file. Long past home time, while keeping focused, then driving exhausted. For three hours sleep, before doing it all again.

The feeling of the knife slashing through your hair, just missing your skin, as the madman screams and hollers in the pitch black street. You arrest, case file, court. The shakes go away three days later. Keep your composure with the now permanently disabled victim though.

The complex fraud investigations, schedule 1 PACE production orders; ripa authorities, police regs, evidential standards; disclosure. Intelligence research, NIM, PPO standards, RTI, offences; definitions, definitions, definitions. UPP, UPA.

My collar, I can tell you, is fucking white and very often covered in blood; whether mine or someone else's. My clock-machine is more imaginary than the copper that Policy Exchange idiot saw on a bus. A bus in his head; the route number 1 to the tooth fairy's house. So, in the best 'blue collar' spirit; why don't you fuck right off? While I write this on the wall in the bogs; you patronising, demeaning wankspanner:

"My collar is white. My uniform is blue. You must be confused. So I'll just say f........"

If I was still a blue collar worker I would have spoken, openly, to you like this from the outset; but I'm not. This has been me mimicking an earlier version of myself; a 17 year old boy who has since grown up, well beyond his years. At least I have the brass ones not to blame it on anyone else.

My blue collar remains in the past; your gutless lack of testes remains in the present. For that reason alone:
You're fired.

The Slip of The Mask:

"it is impossible to keep politics out of politics"

19th of June 2012

Yesterday an event was held in central London, in a plush venue, where even the seats had charging sockets; at least that is, according to one attendee.

It is not in the least unusual for events to take place; nor for speakers to include ministers, corporations or think-tankers. Neither is it unusual for media representatives to attend such well endowed venues. What was unusual, was that the event was a first real outing for Police and Crime Commissioners; the trumpeted saviours of accountability in policing. The particularly unusual thing was the fact that the truth began to out, and due to Social Media; it began to out in real time.

The establishment of 'PCCs' is now law, so can only be stopped by an Act of Parliament and, previously, Chief Officers (at their recent annual conference) were quoted as saying "it was time to SUMO". To borrow from my other blog; this did not mean wrestle with the issue but, rather: Shut Up, Move On. As a Police Officer I can say, without fear of a peer correcting me, that if I walked away from something or blindly accepted it; I wouldn't be doing my duty properly.

At the time Chiefs roared SUMO; PCCs lacked definition.

Yesterday definition is what we got. That recent SUMO roar can only be described, in light of this refinement, as having been premature, verbal ejaculation.

Firstly, at a time of growing public concern over politics and influence, PCCs result in the creation of another layer of political roles; salaries and pensions. This time directly in charge of how your are kept safe in your bed. Imagine if you disagree with the policies but are in the 'perceived problematic minority': how does the potential implication of that sit? Comfortably? I doubt it very much.

Secondly, at a time of unprecedented austerity, when normal people like us are already struggling; when the police service is facing a reduction in budget of 1/5th, despite spelling out how dangerous this is: it has been seen appropriate to introduce a spend of £75 million on this process.

Thirdly, several more worrying facts began to emerge; amongst a backdrop of laughter at the public, that this system is lauded to be in the best interests of. A normal member of the public, a good Christian, was there and walked out because of the offence this mockery caused.

The first real worry came from the revelation that it is seen as unlikely that independent candidates would succeed; so the positions would primarily land in the hands of the main political parties; this was neither surprising nor unexpected. The surprise came in the fact that parties would be able to control PCCs or remove their support if they didn't like the way things were going. This by default has the effect of creating a miniature, Home Office type influence, over local policing; even if the party in question is out of central power. And this, without the balanced board of Police Authority acting as a control measure.

And what if the neighbouring forces are different parties and the party mandate is confrontational or antagonistic? Does mutual assistance grind to a halt, become a battle ground? Crime and Justice Minister, Nick Herbert let his mask slip here, saying "I promised not to be partisan, but..." Thus proving; it is impossible to keep politics out of politics.

The issue of low public turnout was raised as a concern; because a low turnout would mean the person charged with keeping you safe, in your bed, had no real mandate to do so. It was vaguely stated that the minimum turnout "should be like local elections".

I've said it before and will again now; policing is for everyone, equally and without exception. When only a third of the public speak for all, it is unavoidable that people will suffer. In Westminster this seems to neither understood, nor cared about. I noticed the issue of electoral fraud was not raised; when clearly it should have been. The implications of this are huge and you have to ask; why create a local power retention mechanism unless you are convinced you won't have it centrally for long? Food for thought indeed.

Then, the discussion over the Home Secretary's much repeated 'chiefs will be operationally independent'. It seems they will not; the common theme was that PCCs would get straight into tinkering with as much as possible; on the delivery side. Again, my three year old could have seen that coming. Arising from this comes the true horror.

The corporate sponsor of the event, consultancy Deloitte, along with others, made clear that the primary focus of PCCs would be financial. No, not public safety. Money. I hasten to add, that for experts in efficiency and finance; I'm massively surprised they didn't say: "are you sure spending £75 million on this is a good idea in the current climate". Now, why would said consultancy sponsor an event; with access to people eager to tinker and reform? What could they possibly gain? These days I look at Leveson as the tip of the influence iceberg.

Back to the event; in waded G4S and others; clamouring to know 'what could not be privatised'. All the while they rubbed their hands at what could. Herbert's masked slipped completely after this and we got a real glimpse of what's coming. Where a force refuses to 'partner' with a private provider (let's call it privatisation shall we) the implication was that the force would have less officers. Now, I'm sure he meant to say "because they will have to do x, y and z too". Unfortunately what came out was:

   "If you vote John Prescott (who has ruled out privatisation if elected) you will get less officers". It almost sounded like some form of threat to the budget precept.

I don't accept threats, veiled or not.

He, Nick Herbert, also blathered about PCCs being "game changing". I believe this tells us everything we need to know about the Crime and Justice Minister.

a) he thinks policing is a game; not life, death and public safety and;

b) that the real agenda here is to exert political agenda, to secure political longevity and; control.

The latter will be openly used as leverage to push privatisation (still not a rose, even by any other name) into policing; even if the party pushing it comes to lose power nationally. This is the cold, stark, horrifying truth.

I know what PCCs are for; what they have been all along. A back up mechanism, a back door way to secure the private future; for those with vested interests*.

I know that this has been years in the making; that a lot of 'corporate support' has been given and, how this has been done. Just take one look at the Anti Winsor Report. (**10**).

Because I know this, I cannot and will not 'Shut Up and Move On'. Because I'm a police officer and because I have a duty to protect the public, even from politicians if needs be.

I am quite prepared to wrestle.

*On Sunday the 21ˢᵗ of October 2012, the day of
publication of this second edition, *The Telegraph* printed an
article by Andrew Gilligan with the following heading:

  *"A high-profile candidate campaigning to become one of
the Government's new elected Police and Crime
Commissioners is being secretly backed by American neo-
conservative lobbyists and companies pushing for police
privatisation"*. The article can be viewed at:
http://www.telegraph.co.uk/news/politics/9623068/The-
secret-US-lobbyists-behind-Police-and-Crime-
Commissioner-election.html
The same day, one PCC Candidate published a transparency
list, clearly showing direct and indirect approaches made.
This can be viewed at:
http://www.rachelrogers.net/transparency/

Open Letter - Nick Herbert MP:

"as an elected official your sense of public duty
should be sufficiently motivational"

20th of June 2012

Sir,

I am sure that you are incredibly busy, with the events on Police and Crime Commissioners, such as this week's at the Policy Exchange. I am sure you are also 'up to your neck' in your preparations, for your appearance at the Home Affairs Select Committee next Tuesday (the 26th of June 2012); where you will be the first witness.

As many others do, I await with interest to hear the details of the selection process and, your own rationale, for the preferred appointment of locomotive expert, Mr Tom Winsor, as the head of Her Majesty's Inspectorate of Constabulary. I wish you the very best of luck, in coming across well.

In the meantime, I do have questions, relevant to the steps being taken to privatise policing; I believe you now prefer to call this 'partnering'. I cannot blame you for attempting to avoid the perceived, negative image of the former, in favour of the more media friendly latter.

I would very much appreciate it if you, as the Minister for Crime and Justice, could take the time to reply. As this is an open letter; I will also of course post your reply openly. In order that all parties who are worrying, can have their concerns alleviated as quickly as possible.

1) It seems, from the event this week, that it was sponsored by consultancy Deloitte. Tell me what their interest was? I am aware that you have a good relationship with the Exchange and your former Staff Officer Blair Gibbs, so he may be able to provide you with additional information should you need it to reply effectively. And, tell me how much did Deloitte contribute to the event? Please also explain your relationship with the Policy Exchange and how this has influenced you in mapping out police reform; if at all.

2) What is your knowledge of 'ADS' and their function in representing the interests of numerous corporations in security? What was their interest in sponsoring the recent policing futures event? How much did they contribute, financially, to the event?

3) Including your time at Reform, how much contact have you had with G4S? Please try and be specific. Were G4S or other companies such as Serco making any kind of financial contribution to Reform? If so, how much, from

when exactly and, how regularly. If you could again clarify why they contribute, that would be of great help in explaining this.

4) Please outline in detail your personal experience as regards to policing.

These are initial questions and I hope that you are able to be clear and swift in your reply. I am if course aware that you have no obligation to provide responses; but as an elected official your sense of public duty should be sufficiently motivational. As of course you are aware, the police are the public too.

The Rules of Engagement:

"we will hold our line"

23rd of June 2012

There is one simple rule, above all others that I
have been taught; not only as a police officer
but long before too. That rule is: Never run to a
fight.

Before you fight, you have to make sure that
you must fight, that there is no other way and;
make sure that you see where the danger lies.
Up until now I have been strolling; taking in
what's happening. Looking to see where the
danger lies. Now, I've reached that moment,
where I know I must fight; my heart is
pounding even at the thought. This will be the
most dangerous fight I have ever taken on. I do
know, that I don't stand alone. I also know that
if ever there was a right reason to fight, this is
it.

The police is a service for the public and now,
through cause of selfishness, agenda and greed
it stands on the brink of destruction. The
service, a service for all of us, will be
politicised, privatised and perverted. This is
being done with malice aforethought. There is
just no way that I can dress it up.

I have an overview of what the reasons for this
are, I have more than enough suspicion to
consider it reasonable. But, now, the fight is

only moments away and I must make sure, one last time, that I (and anyone else who decides to stand with me), have a full understanding of the rules of engagement. The obligation of duty to every police officer in England and Wales is laid down in law.

Section 29 of the Police Act 1996 is the latest incarnation of this that compels every new member of a police force to attest by making a declaration. As we all know from The Last Call to Attention I prefer the more historic version but the current Schedule makes the oath of attestation as follows:

"I do solemnly and sincerely declare and affirm that I will well and truly serve the Queen in the office of constable, with fairness, integrity, diligence and impartiality; upholding fundamental human rights and according equal respect to all people; and that I will, to the best of my power, cause the peace to be kept and preserved and prevent all offences against people and property, and that while I continue to hold the said office I will, to the best of my skill and knowledge, discharge all the duties thereof faithfully according to law".

Once bound by this oath, Section 50 of the same act binds officers to regulations set by the Secretary of State. One set of these are the

Police (Conduct) Regulations 2008, which contain a schedule of behaviours to which officers must adhere to. These behaviours include:

Honesty and Integrity:
Police Officers are honest, act with integrity and do not compromise or abuse their position.

Orders and Instructions:
Police officers only give and carry out lawful orders and instructions.

Discreditable Conduct:
Police officers behave in a manner which does not discredit the police service or undermine public confidence in it, whether on or off duty.

Challenging and Reporting Improper Conduct:
Police officers report, challenge or take action against the conduct of colleagues which has fallen below the standards of professional behaviour.

Ministers are bound, as another type of public office holder, in much the same way, by the Ministerial Code 2010.
Under Common Law, if a public officer wilfully and without reasonable excuse or

justification neglects to perform any duty they are bound to perform, by Common Law or Statute, then they are guilty of the offence of misconduct in a public office. The elements of this offence are that:

a) a public officer was acting as such
b) wilfully neglected to perform their duty and/or
c) wilfully misconducted themselves in a way which amounted to an abuse of the public's trust in the office holder
d) without reasonable excuse or justification

The misconduct is not restricted to dishonesty, bribery or corruption but must injure the public interest and call for condemnation and punishment. For example in the case of R v Dynham [1979] a police officer watched a man being beaten but did not intervene; the officer was convicted.

A further Common Law offence is called Perverting the Course of Justice and is committed where a person embarks on a course of conduct, which has a tendency to, and was intended to, pervert the course of public justice. The ways in which this can be committed include; concealing offences, assisting others to evade arrest and failing to prosecute.

The Police Act 1996 once again make a further provision of note, in Section 89(2). It states that any person who resists or wilfully obstructs a constable in the execution of his duty, or a person assisting a constable in the execution of his duty, shall be guilty of an offence. And another in Section 30, which defines the jurisdiction of a Constable as: "throughout England and Wales and the adjacent United Kingdom waters".

So, in summary: The rules are that I must act; that if I don't I break the law. The rules are that no-one should stand in my way; if they do, they break the law.

These rules apply to every single officer in the country. These are the rules of engagement; the rules of this particular fight. Of final interest is Section 91, which provides for an offence of causing disaffection. According to legal digests the offence is "basically encouraging dissatisfaction amongst members of the police force or seducing any member of the force from his duty of allegiance to the Crown".

As a last note I'd like to say, to make it clear, that I and all the officers (and supporters) who come together on Twitter, under the collective groups #AntiWinsorNetwork and

#HoldTheLine and others; have spread a huge amount of affection for the service, for the very office that the rules apply to. We together are the very definition of 'anti-disaffection'. Collectively we are fighting to preserve the office of Constable and, the conditions and regulations that come with it; not only that, but we are locked in a battle with many who are openly trying to force and seduce us away from our allegiance to the Crown, into a political world of profit.

No matter how hard they try, no matter how prolonged their attempts to succeed; we will hold our line. Despite their continued efforts, we will not be disaffected from our service or our duty and a day may come when we remind them of Section 91 of the Police Act 1996; with words from another piece of legislation, PACE. The Codes of Practice, Code G, Paragraph 3.5 says:

"You do not have to say anything. But it may harm your defence if you do not mention when questioned something which you later rely on in court. Anything you do say may be given in evidence".

United we stand behind the oath that binds us; and, now that the rules of engagement are clear: the Office of Constable is ready to fight.

The Freedom of Expression:

"We must uphold the law and preserve human rights"

24th of June 2012

The Human Rights Act is often shown much disdain, because of how it is interpreted. At one stage or another most people have had a good moan about it; but then, we often forget, it is that very act the enshrines our right to do just that:

"Article 10, Freedom of Expression of the Human Rights Act 1998, which is a qualified right, states everyone has the right of freedom of expression. This right shall include freedom to hold opinions and to receive and impart information and ideas without interference by public authority and regardless of frontiers. This guarantees the right to pass information to other people and to receive information that other people want to give to you. It also guarantees the right to hold and express opinions and ideas."

You want to speak, you speak. You want to tweet, you tweet. You want to share, you share and you cannot be interfered with. Is that a right you want rid of? Think carefully because; it might seem nice while it is someone else who doesn't have it...but if you find yourself silenced?

The new laws on trolling come dangerously close to a removal of this but, because the word troll has been used, it has almost been hidden from sensible, rational minds. Made titillating.

Imagine you are passionate about something and want to speak your mind about it; say policing. Because the topic is sensitive and, because there is a distinct probability of backlash or attack from a number of self preserving parties: you choose to do so anonymously to protect, not just yourself, but your family.

Imagine, that even with Article 10 in place, there are some in public office who would be so perturbed by your success in doing so; that they would threaten your anonymity in order to try and force you to stop. Imagine worse still if they did it with glee. In the future, you the anonymous party, may have no protection at all. But...that is the future and it isn't here yet. For now you, whether named or anonymous are protected by Article 10 so speak on and; speak out safely.

The act itself says:
   "It is unlawful for a public authority to act in a way which is incompatible with a "Convention Right". A person who claims that a public authority has acted (or proposes to act) in a way which is unlawful under the Human

Rights Act 1998 may, if he or she is (or would
be) a victim of the unlawful act either:
Bring proceedings in any appropriate court or
tribunal against the authority under the Human
Rights Act 1998; or
rely on the Convention right concerned in any
legal proceedings."

Now imagine that the person gleefully trying to
expose you worked for a national, public body,
dedicated to the improvement of, lets say,
policing. Imagine, worse still that they had 30
years experience as a police officer, before
becoming a national advisor, to police forces,
on digital engagement. And finally, imagine
that all of this was taking place on Twitter, one
of the biggest successes in digital media.

Not only would this person, by virtue of 30
years experience in policing know what they
were doing was morally wrong; not only would
they know it reflected poorly on them and their
employer; not only would it fly in the face of
Article 10, of which they are well aware...but
that if they were doing it out of some kind of
perverse amusement? Practically pledging to
continue with a:

;)

Lastly; what if they had been told, clearly and bluntly to stop? But actively chose to continue. What then? Well, thankfully for now, the rules of engagement for police officers are clear: we must uphold the law and preserve human rights and we must challenge inappropriate behaviour. If I was this imaginary person; I'd be thinking on that very carefully.

I'd be checking that my understanding of the harassment act was up to date; that I knew the implications of breaching a human right. That I had considered if such continued behaviour in a public office (for that's what it is in this imagining) could amount to an abuse of public trust; by breaching that human right or threatening to. Even if the threat was veiled I'd want to make sure I'd understood alarm and distress; how they can be caused.
If I was that imaginary person AND I had been told bluntly; I would be walking away.

The beauty of Article 10 is that I can write this imaginary scenario and pass it around. That right is preserved for me and because of my own promise; I will go to the ends of the earth to preserve it for others.

Open Email - Tom Winsor:

"the frustration boils until it has something to aim at"

27th of June 2012

Sir,

You may be startled by this but, on behalf of the police, I would like very much to welcome you into your new position.

I know it is yet to be finally ratified but, I am sure you are ready (as we are) to get started.

As well as welcome you, I would like to talk to you about the #AntiWinsorNetwork. To make clear some points; before they are lost in the muddied waters. I have thus far left the word 'dreaded' out, as the hash tag is little more than an established communication channel; allowing a group of people, both police and public, to speak to each other in the hundreds. Think of it as little more than a press of the conference call button.

That really is all it is used for; rather than some weapon of 'disgraceful' vilification; as some would have us believe. The name itself, as far as we are concerned, refers to the 'nickname' of the report 'Winsor 2', rather than yourself, as a person, directly.

That report generates many real concerns in officers and, as a result, you have become the physical embodiment of that concern. A lack of communication from our leadership has only fuelled the worry; by leaving question marks hanging open in the air. We know this experience intimately; as officers are the physical embodiment of the state and, often, subject to public fury. You, us...the end result is always the same; the frustration boils until it has something to aim at. This is simple human psychology rather than malice and; certain parties above us, have been only too happy to bait the bear. Knowing full well that the frustrations would be directed at you, as that manifestation. I have found that realisation particularly saddening.

Humans are simple creatures of passion; easy to wound, quick to vent. With 32 years in legal practice you will know this and nod in agreement I am sure.

The primary concerns over the report are not (and haven't really ever been) about pay. That must be made loud and clear; once and for all. There are questions over the police pension situation but the concerns are, in the majority:

1) That officers already pay the most in the public sector; which dents the monthly budget during tight times. This impacts on families;

children. Further increases are the concern. (This does not relate to your report but amplifies the effect of other perceived changes).

and;

2) That police officers in their sixties will be operationally wrecked, due to the cumulative effects of shift work, Post Traumatic Stress Disorder, exposure to disease and dangerous situations. The concern is that the mind would be willing but the body would inevitably fail in the duty to protect the public.

This sits well with no police officer, nor with any member of the public I have spoken to. Officers are concerned at compulsory redundancy; not because we feel we should be exempt - despite having already waived industrial rights to serve our communities - but because we fear mismanagement. Abuse. Agenda. We fear that the quick fix culture, embedded through the change for promotion culture, will result in misguided or selfish use of the facility. We fear it would be used to allow privatisation contracts to take hold; for the sworn officers to be reduced to such a number, that use of force will have to become the primary option due to lack of tactical support. This is the reality of the escalation scale and, at present, the risk of public protest and disorder is increasing daily.

We worry that the sworn element of policing will be forced to become the Orwellian boot that stamps the face. We do not want this for our service, we want the whole public to be proud of us; not fear or hate us.

These are the real concerns of officers; for their husbands, wives, children; the public they serve. None of us put our lives on hold, take this grave and responsibility laden oath of service, for money. We do it because we want to make society better; we want to keep criminals off the street. We want no more victims. This is not my most eloquent email but, I hope this clarifies somewhat; what the #antiwinsornetwork is in reality.

In any case, you are an intelligent man; we've had no doubts about your ability to see through spin. I like to think that you would actually take heart in the passion and fight that has been displayed. That you are reassured in the knowledge that officers will question, will challenge. Will not blindly and nonchalantly accept the word of any person. That you see officers who will not back down until facts are clear, that engage at all levels of society.

We have been bulldogs in this process, there are no easy rides with us.

Now you know that there are officers like us out there; just imagine how tenaciously we fight crime for the public. Imagine how robust we are a challenging impropriety within the service. I challenge you not to feel safer in that knowledge. Many of the public who have engaged with us are proud to have discovered this too. Many of them had ceased to believe it. The oath is something special and people have been reminded of that. We reminded them of that.

Once again, welcome to the police; a service for the public, made of the public. A place were the difficult questions cannot, will not and should not be ignored. I feel confident that you will fit right in.

Open Email - Nick Herbert:

"please calm down, for everyone's sake"

28th of June 2012

Sir,

I note that, as yet, I have had no reply to my email dated the 21st of June 2012. This is quite regrettable.

I am also informed by supportive members of the public that, in your own constituency, a disabled group is still waiting for a response after their third letter. They advised me not to hold my breath but; I live in infinite hope.

In that line of thought, I hope that there is not some pattern of behaviour in this; that would be disappointing. Had this been a MOPC (*Mayor's Office for Policing and Crime*) mystery shop, of a Safer Neighbourhood Team (*SNT*), this would have resulted in a contact failure report. Perhaps there is a communications issue which any SNT would be happy to help you with. Public confidence and satisfaction is of course central in both our lines of public duty.

My original questions still stand, however I am compelled to turn to other, no less serious matters. This is me, speaking to you as a normal bloke, openly, frankly.

Your deeply cynical attack on police officers at the Home Affairs Select Committee was a very poor show. Deeply disappointing. Clearly there is something, about Police Officers challenging you, which gets under your skin; you have what poker players would call a tell. In your case it manifests as fluster, Freudian slip and attack.

I often wonder, going all the way back to your House of Commons 'C' word incident; what is the exact nature of your issue? Maybe you could reflect upon that and proffer an explanation if you arrive at one. A trip around the reflective learning cycle can never do harm.

At the HASC you saw fit to discuss 'tweeting' officers and singled out a group as a disgrace. You singled out a hash tag, the #AntiWinsorNetwork. You continued in your persistence that the only issue was pay. That it was a minority of disgruntled and disgraceful officers. Because you have been irritated, riled as those working with you put it, you have failed to look past your own assumption; you have been blinded by anger. The red mist. As a serving police officer I would be happy to share some techniques with you, to avoid any further, embarrassing or damaging repeats of this.

What you haven't seen through the mist is, that large numbers of members of the public support the #AntiWinsorNetwork. Because it doesn't stand for pay; it stands for public engagement, reminds officers and the public alike, that the service is for them; made up of them. It stands against elements of a report, bearing a man's name, that facilitate other change in the service. That clear the path for companies to take over functions for the public, for profit. It stands against the wilful and reckless, final politicisation of the police.

It stands for public safety. It stands to allow people to vent their impossibly pent up worries. It stands for support, unlikely friendship, humour and healthy debate. It stands for being human, being real; being truly part of the public that we serve.

It was very easy for you to make a water muddying hoo-ha, calculated I reasonably believe, to drive your message into the media. To generate public disgust, to dent confidence and satisfaction. To cause a knee jerk reaction, by Chief Officers, to silence tweeting officers. This is the base principle of spin and media management is it not? Present a message that will cause others to take action; or simply react in a predictable way.

My concern is that it is widely known at the Home Office that you are angry; that you do not like police officers, or their public supporters, laying challenging questions upon you. This is no apparent secret. Has it come already to the point where you demand to know why officers are allowed to tweet? Demand it stopped? I believe that conversation has taken place.

I suspect, not unreasonably, that Professional Standards departments will be receiving new guidelines soon. The very thought of wilfully restricting Article 10 rights, freedom of expression, out of anger...well...it's Orwellian isn't it? This goes well beyond acceptable. You display your anger even in your letters to the Federation.

You are angry and it is seemingly impairing your judgement, clouding your decision making. You hold the safety of the whole public in your hands; this is no weight to carry lightly, flippantly or in rage. You should take a step back. You must calm down.

It's good to talk and, every conversation comes to an end; so to conclude:

1) Could the reply please be provided to my original email.

2) Can you please stop your attempts, by spin and other routes, to silence anyone who asks uncomfortable or difficult questions.

and;

3) Can you please calm down, for everyone's sake.

The Question of Nepotism:

"a problem shared is a problem halved"

2nd July 2012

I've had my eyes opened repeatedly over recent weeks, not least of all to exactly how much information is available, openly, on the Internet. It's vast.

You can't beat a little conversation though, especially when people, who truly know what they are talking about, say things like "basically the whole thing is corrupt, pass Chief Inspector and it's definitely who you know and, what you are willing to do for them". I particularly enjoyed being told "if you aren't prepared to network, even when you aren't comfortable with it, you just can't get on, that's just how it works and it's sad".

I enjoyed this for two reasons. Firstly it confirms to a large degree what I've long suspected and secondly that I've been right for some time; that the problems in the police lie in the 'networks' at the top. By design.

Even 'by design' I say with a sense of irony, Safer by Design is one of the key 'products' of ACPO Crime Prevention Initiatives Ltd.

The networks potentially explain a lot about the silence from ACPO and ties in with comments made by Baroness Doocey when she spoke to

Elizabeth Filkin. She was adamant the focus should be upwards. It also makes me chuckle because I look to our future leaders, the High Potential Development Scheme 'flyers' and see that many of them are great at networking, yet pretty mediocre or worse at police work. In fact I'd go so far as to say that they are, at least in part, groomed to network rather than police. I went for the scheme this year, out of curiosity; to satisfy my own thoughts.

It's my business to know how things work after all and I set no boundaries on topic. I rigidly stuck to police work, backed up by my commended history and excellent PDR (*Professional Development Review*) record. I wrote the reasons the feedback would give for non acceptance out in advance and, howled with laughter when it came back almost word for word; plus the addition of spelling mistakes.

If police work is secondary and your ability to be groomed, to network, is essential; then I remain relieved that my face doesn't fit and; I can walk even taller than I did before. The scheme has become a parody of the "basically corrupt" networking I had explained, candidly, to me.

There is a word, which springs to mind:
nepotism
Noun
The practice among those with power or influence of favouring relatives or friends, esp. by giving them jobs.

And that, leads me into another most curious discussion, which oddly combines the vast resource of the Internet and a good old fashioned chat.

I received an anonymous email (as I am prone to having put my head above the parapet) and the content is a little disturbing if accurate; which it seems to be. If you can confirm different, let me know and I'll post the clarification straight away.

But first, a quick reminder:
1) Sir Edward M Crew had a vote of no confidence by staff when he led West Midlands Police and retired in 2004. He is now a patron at ADS, a company which provides a network for security companies. He also appears listed with consultancy Team Assure.
2) Chris Sims is now the chief of West Midlands and with Lynne Owens of Surrey, a huge tender has been put out for 'privatised' services. Among the networks at the top, this is now referred to as partnering or outsourcing.

3) Sir Edward Crew was principle advisor to Tom Winsor during his independent review. Elements of that report are now thought to be a 'copy' of an earlier David Cameron speech and it seems elements written by Mr Winsor had to be checked by the Home Office, to make sure they were 'On Target'.

4) The Winsor report is largely understood to be a financial mechanism which ultimately facilitates greater 'partnering' and the new remit of HMIC, to which Tom Winsor is to be appointed head, has value for money and partnering at the heart.

Recap complete; here is what I was sent:

"Lynne Gillian CREW, born Jan, Feb or Mar 1969 in Sutton, Surrey, showing mothers maiden name as GLOVER. The marriage register of Gillian W. GLOVER to Edward M CREW, is shown in the Surrey South Eastern District. In October 1990, Lynne G CREW married Simon G NANKIVELL in Kent, however, in September 1995, Lynne Gillian NANKIVELL married David Neil OWENS. Hence Lynne G CREW to Lynne G OWENS (She actually looks like him too). On her bio which was from an interview this year, she states she is 43 years old (therefore accurate with Lynne Gillian CREW date of birth being Jan, Feb or Mar 1969 as shown in birth register), she makes reference to her husband, 'Neil', as having left his job as a Police Officer to look after their daughter."

David Neil Owens is shown as director of a residents association in Surrey on the free company check services.
    "This is the link to probably the most comprehensive bio Owens has on the internet (**11**)"

In the bio it mentions her dedicated police family.
    "This is the link to a Kent Police museum site with a photograph of Edward M CREW, from his time there, with a very small history of his postings (**12**)
This link is from the Guardian and shows the full name of Lynn Gillian OWENS as receiving the QPM in the 2008 New Years Honours list. (**13**)"

In the same list is that McPherson fellow, the 'Freebie King' who went from Norfolk to the Met, then disappeared to KPMG just after the riots.
    "Here are the links to bios of Edward Crew and Chris Sims which show that Sims worked under him when Crew was CC in West Midlands (**14 & 15**). And here is a document,

which outlines some of the roles that W/Mids and Surrey have put out to tender (**16**). Interestingly 'lot 1', as they call it, states that the list is not exhaustive and 'consideration' may be given to including additional services, or services of a similar nature. 'Lot 1' includes:

"investigate crimes, detain suspects (custody services is a separate lot), investigate incidents, manage major incidents, patrol neighbourhoods, manage high risk individuals, disrupt criminal networks".

Both current chiefs have promised to preserve the office of Constable. This tender does not read that way. Or, in the words of my anonymous friend: "my arse".

So, there it is. I start with nepotism and a recap...I find at the end I'm as deeply concerned as ever about the Winsor report, ACPO and, in fact, this whole reform agenda for policing. I thank the anonymous sender for the email; it was truly enlightening and good to see that people are increasingly speaking out and raising their concerns. That is not only healthy but; necessary.

As my Nan always said; a problem shared is a problem halved. I'll leave you all to draw your own conclusions and as ever, discuss and debate; openly and honestly. For me, yet more questions are raised than are answered and; this rabbit hole is turning out to be quite deep indeed.

The Smell of Success:

"It's cosier than the Dormouse's teapot at the Mad
Hatter's tea party"

3rd of July 2012

Oh dear. My nostrils are filled with the smell of something...could it be success? Money? No. It's a rather unpleasant pong wafting from G4S.

I have been sent some real gems today, you see; and the pungent aroma arrived with them. First I am told that G4S have been replaced by The Army, in doing the security entry posts at the Olympic Park. I can't confirm or deny that as I haven't been there myself but then I received these two links:

   "First (longest) vid: (**17**)

   Second vid: (**18**)"

That's right, someone has gone undercover at G4S and, well..you decide; I'm not sure that smell is success at all. Another 'S' entirely.

Then to put chocolate sprinkles on my day, the anonymous friend was back; you know, the one with a penchant for family trees. But first, as is routine, a reminder:

1) G4S pay into Reform, the think tank started by Crime and Justice Minister Nick Herbert.
2) The new role of the HMIC will be to ensure Value For Money and encourage the use of partnering arrangements; or privatisation as we humans like to call it.
and;

3) G4S already are cutting jobs at Lincolnshire, one of the three 'endangered' forces as defined by Sir Dennis O'Connor yesterday. G4S were of course represented in the £200 million contract by White and Case, the law firm in which Tom Winsor is and was a partner while writing his report.

Without further ado:
   "This is from the G4S media page of their website: (**19**) It relates to the Prime Ministers Trade Mission to Africa in July 2011.

As well as the smiling PM and other ministers, the third person to the right of the PM as you look at the picture, standing slightly back from the front row and wearing a dark suit and light blue tie is David Taylor-Smith (chief executive, G4S Security Services UK and Ireland).

The third paragraph of the article includes a quote from David Taylor-Smith "we look forward to the Prime Minister's support in helping British companies to compete even more effectively."

Now this obviously relates to the trade mission, but everything that is happening in the UK suggests that it may not have only been Africa where deals have been struck."

I see, do you readers? It's cosier than the Dormouse's teapot at the Mad Hatter's tea party. Hi Dave, Hi Dave. Love you Dave, Love you Dave. Maybe.

This article is from 20th June 2012 in the Guardian (**20**). It relates to David Taylor-Smith and the headline reads:
   "G4S chief predicts mass police privatisation - Private companies will be running large parts of the police service within five years, according to security firm head". Why is he so confident.?"
Ooh, me, me!! My hand is up, I know the answer! Is it because he too knows how nepotism works? Maybe.
   "This next link is the profile of David Taylor-Smith which is from June 2007 (**21**). There is no doubting that he has successfully expanded the business, but this shows that it really is all about the money".

In the words of my nan, in Tesco, as she went senile: 'no fucking shit. Where are the condoms Malcolm?'. (Just seemed apt).

Then on the G4S website under Capital Markets Day is a PDF document:

"Written by David Taylor-Smith relating to the Africa and UK markets. It is an essential read and shows how G4S are taking over masses of Government related posts. Slide 17 - Market Opportunity only for contracts in excess of £3 million shows they are looking at 92% of their business being from Government and only 8% from commercial sector.

It outlines their relevant strategies including further developing their BPO capability. They have their fingers all over NHS, DWP, Police, Prisons...Banking."

NHS, Police....he said Banking? But wasn't this chap teapot cosy with the PM too a few paragraphs ago. My spider sense is tingling.

"I've included this link as well, although I did briefly push it out there last week so you are probably aware of it. The ex Chief Constable of Lincolnshire Richard Crompton, who brokered the G4S deal for their force gets a job as chairman on Portsmouth NHS Trust (**22**). As the G4S, PDF shows, they are all over the NHS already, but here is a link to one of their previous job adverts (**23**)".

So, was this chief's palm greased for opening the door to G4S at Lincolnshire? Now there's a question; and not one I can answer. I seem to remember the Chairman of G4S however, describing the Lincolnshire deal as 'Market Changing'. (see The Office of Constable Rises series on YouTube and watch Part 3). That's a direct quote.

"Oh, one final thing, G4S current advert for HR Director in their Government and Outsourcing Services, note the salary, 6 figure plus generous benefits. Tax payers will be paying that."

Well, if we stand here in a few months time and that salary still looks set to be paid by the public purse; then we have waved the white flag and run to the hills.

But I smell something and it isn't the smell of success...I have never backed away from odour yet; even the ones that set off my gag reflex. Fortunately I stand, not in the mood for running and...I do not stand alone.

Open Email to Nick Herbert

"I would like a word with you"

listen; genuinely listen.

Firstly, let's talk about drops in numbers and no, you can't use the 'front line' as a diversion. You have constantly shown that you have little concept of what it is; hugely disappointing for the Crime and Justice Minister.

It seems the most accurate figures, as referred to in The Economist, are an overall loss to the service of 32,400 of which approximately 15,000 will be officers. The reality is, that's half of the Met. Gone. With more cuts to bite, it seems to have become apparent in recent days, that the Met itself is preparing to drop between 6,500 and 8,000 officers. That's about half the number it took to quell the riots, or if you prefer the whole of Greater Manchester Police. Gone.

When you started out there were 143,000 and already it is down to around 135,000. Just off the top of my head, these are pretty much the Home Office figures. 600 recruits at Hendon will not fix this and I hasten to remind you that, under new recruitment plans, they were either Specials, PCSOs or DDOs beforehand anyway. The point being, they were already part of our resilience so you have gained no strength, just moved it.

So let's be clear. A reduction is a cut. Juggling is not and increase. You cannot play the ball under the cup game with the safety of the public so, forthwith, please stop trying.

The lady on Channel 4, who you were so very clearly annoyed with, was right: the cut is a broken election promise. Clear as day. Even reverting to the 'front line' defence you say; it's 6%, only 6%, not a cut. Well, I may not be a master of mathematics but 100 minus 6 is 94. That is less 'frontline', therefore, by definition a reduction; in slang, a cut. No wriggle, no spin.

I note you again trumpet the increase in neighbourhood team numbers; again this is just juggling. taking officers from one place and putting them in another. You're making this look almost like an art now. The model of larger neighbourhood teams and smaller response teams was, I believe, pioneered by Ian McPherson QPM at Norfolk before he went to the Met. It is a model which has been widely duplicated. The key is to reduce response teams and 'squads' and place the surplus in larger, local policing teams. Local policing teams who work between eight o'clock in the morning and midnight.

May I take this opportunity to point out that

Winsor 1, by adding the 10% allowance payment between 2000 hours and 0600 hours has now practically forced all forces to make this move; due to the additional, financial pressure placed upon them. The local model therefore keeps cost down for chiefs and, allows you to say that neighbourhood teams are expanding.

What a lovely piece of PR that must be to have in your pocket.

That's fine and dandy but ask yourself; once McPherson began this, starting with shifts in London, how many police officers were on the street, on the first night of the riots? It was 3300 or thereabouts. About 10% of the workforce. At a peak time. We know it took days to mobilise the force because of shift pattern chaos arising from the changes and; eventually it took 16,000 officers on the street to stop the disorder.

You are forcing this to become a default position for all forces.

The riots cost £370 million with around £100 million of that being on the overtime needed to rectify the situation brought on by exactly the kind of arrangement you are pushing. Next time it will also cost 10% more.

I cannot begin to imagine the ill conceived thought process you have gone through but must ask you, once again; to get a grip of reality. You are playing a game with something that is not a toy; public safety. I know you want to take officers from 'back office' roles to bolster your perverse version of the front line and you expect 'partnering' to solve this. Noone is comfortable with this, not least because of the open question marks of large corporations lobbying parliament and influencing politicians. Not even the huge G4S showcase event of the Olympics will ever be enough to address the concerns. We do give you full marks for having a try though.

I noted with huge interest your proud fanfare about response times being maintained. That is largely down to the dedication of Response Team officers but - and there is a but - you haven't really been that honest there, have you?

What you failed to mention (and you had ample opportunity) was that almost all forces have had to elongate response times. Most immediate responses are up from from 10 or 12 minutes to 15 or 20 minutes. Most priority calls are now within an hour, up from 30 minutes in some cases. Some forces now have a priority response time of 1-3 hours. You see, in reality, in truth, the goal posts have been moved to meet the ball. Maybe you should publicly clarify this.

Maybe you should play the ball, not the goal posts.

You also continue to bang on about crime reduction. It's easy to achieve when you have people dedicated to eliminating crime figures, to the massage of figures. In some cases people spend more time convincing the public a crime doesn't need recording than they would investigating it.

The targets culture has never had a place in policing so; maybe it's time for a different approach. For a week why don't forces record all reported crime so we can see what the actual problem looks like. I say this not because it will simply destroy your cynical argument but: Because it will also, for the first time in years, allow chiefs to see where their resource is actually needed. You talk yourself about resource distribution. You can't get it right if a problem is hidden. This is simple policing, maybe you should try it and, I'd be more than happy to advise you.

You have much growing up to do, much to

learn. You have a temper which needs to be addressed and you have a particular penchant for half truth. As Mark Twain said:

"There are lies, damn lies and statistics".

If you continue to use all three you stand to become one of the most dangerous people I have ever come across. Do not continue to put the public at risk; you have duties and responsibilities as laid out in the ministerial code. You have a real opportunity to prove yourself and an exigency of duty to come clean to both the police and the public they serve.

It's important you face up to this now, now, before it is too late and I simply cannot apologise for spelling it out so bluntly. Maybe it's exactly what you need.

Maybe, probably, you will ignore this, maybe you will keep cutting; keep adding risk. In which case I'm sure David Copperfield will be in touch, to ask advice on how to make very large things disappear.

The Truth About Anger:

"if this message continues to be lost, to be spun; the
sense of duty behind it will be buried forever"

6th July 2012

It's been a busy old week, not least dealing with two very young, pox ridden children. I was going to be taking them to the West Country to see their Aunt and Cousin but:
a) I've seen 28 Days Later. This is how it starts. and;
b) The local shops are all out of little bells that they could ring.

Instead they are being repeatedly smothered in a pink lotion and the youngest is being dosed up with Calpol to control her fever. All the while the not so big brother is finding new ways to empty his boxes of toys across the entire house.

Outside provides no escape as there is rain and wetness. Generally a bad thing for ill children (although my Nan would have slapped some wellies on me and dragged my sorry behind up the High Street, all those years ago). Subsequently, not so big brother is becoming increasingly frustrated; which brings me on to the topic of anger.

Anger

noun
A strong feeling of displeasure or hostility.

I firmly believe that the media at large are fully aware of how angry police officers are, in fact I'm fairly sure the anger they see is an emotive one they haven't seen before. I believe that this anger is a significant element that is being taken into consideration in the reporting, or indeed non-reporting, of the issues surrounding police reform. I think it is high noon for this issue. For it to be resolved once and for all.

There is much spin, much put into the public domain that is designed to make people think the anger from police officers is purely about pay and pensions. It simply isn't, that's a very small part of it and not for the selfish 'pay-packet' reasons portrayed. The absolute beauty of Social Media is the fast response you can get to questions and, as a copper, I can tell you that the faster the speed of reply, the more honesty it contains. Here are some comments from today:

"I am angry because of the way that we as police officers are being walked over by this government as there is absolutely nothing we can do. The rail workers, bus drivers etc can strike and are using this to great effect. However to be promised things 21 years ago and now to be told I will have my pay cut, my pension changed etc and there is nothing I can do makes me furious. On top of this is the effect this is having on the service we can provide and that the response officers, like myself, that remain are being stretched to breaking point. Dangerous for us, our families and the public at large."

"I am angry because I joined what used to be a great Police Service. We stood up for what was right and I used to feel like I was making a difference. Politics now plays for too bigger a role in policing and with resources diminishing fast I can no longer stand up for what is right. We have become puppets to politicians."

"Why Angry?? Because we don't have enough resources, the right kit, or enough of it. Not enough resources. Goes without saying. We're constantly running around chasing our tails. Every department is short staffed. And more cuts in officers and staff to come. The tipping point is fast approaching. Turned in for work the other day and had 6 officers out of 12 immediately detached elsewhere. No resilience. There will come a time in the near future where we will no longer be able to provide anything that resembles a service. Clothing is sub-standard and generally not fit for purpose. IT system woefully needs updating upgrading. Increases time in station as everything is so slow. The Vauxhall Astras we have are worse than useless. Slow, underpowered and have no KRS (key-less running system). Hopeless for getting anywhere quickly, and if lights needed whilst static (road block etc) have to be with it at all times as keys have to be while running."

"I am angry because I am being handcuffed by a Government who want to make policing "profitable" at the expense of public safety. As a police officer one of my roles is to make my community safe and for them to feel safe. If I don't feel safe because there are insufficient colleagues on duty to assist me or I don't have the appropriate equipment to protect myself or the public how can I be expected to achieve this? The Federation have tried to get the government to understand our message but they refuse to listen to us."

"For nigh on 30 years I've given my life to the job. Missed my daughters grow up, parents evenings, birthdays, scans, the list is endless. I've done it as at those times the public needed me more. To stand by my oath, to make a difference to those in need. Yes, the job is well paid, but its not enough for what we do, nothing is. But none of us do it just for the money. To see it being dismantled for the sake of others profit hurts me, angers me. But to have those people lie to the public by saying I'm greedy &

its only about my wages makes me livid. No seriously it does. I could easily do someone harm over it. My colleagues, well there is a few who are standing up to this. But the remainder don't feel any less, they're just scared to say so for the sake of getting in trouble and losing their job. I have also have a son who is 2. I saw him on Monday morning at 9am and not again till Thursday at 5pm. I was working umpteen hours, day & night to keep the public safe. To keep guns & bombs off our streets. My daughters are older & know the truth. One day, their dad may not come home because he's had to stand near to a bomber to point them out to a firearms team, if they get there quickly enough. Chances are even if they get there on time, it will still go bang. I don't do this for money, I do it to protect the public and the future for us all, including my kids and yours. Don't lie to the public about your agenda and don't you dare tell them I'm protesting because I'm greedy. You may now understand a little of my anger."

"The calculated & political targeting of a public service who have relatively few defenders & little power to voice their concerns."

"The "reform" is an attack. Ideological change, ignorance of role and requirements will not help. Privatisation is a big nail..."

"I'm scared they may pave the way for the privatisation of something that should remain independent & not answerable to shareholders"

"I want effective police that serve everyone equally. Not minimum wage mercenary's serving MPs interests"

"Poor un-evidenced report conning public, taking away independence,policing for profit leading to a soul-less uncaring service."

"The downright corruption behind it. Because it means that the public will not get the service they deserve. Full stop"

The themes that run through are quite clear.

Hopelessness is common, arising from the fact that officers sacrifice their industrial rights and subsequently voice in order to serve the public. Officers want to serve the public not politics and certainly don't want policing to be about profit.

Resilience is frequently mentioned and we'd all do well to remember that this is 'pre' the bulk of the cuts. If officers on the ground are stretched now, what does this tell you about further reductions? Equipment is also mentioned yet is largely left out of the reform agenda, when clearly it could produce mass savings and improvements. The problem is, only those who do the job can fully understand a lot of this and that lack of understanding is also a factor.

All of this combines to create frustration and, the constant talking to a perceived wall, is what has lead (and is leading) to anger. Like many others, I'd be better off under the Winsor proposals, yet I stand and fight them anyway, not out of anger about pay...that would be madness...but because this is about much more. It's about a service that some of us want to see made as it should be; rather than destroyed by people who blankly refuse to listen. Or who serve their own agenda. The difference in the case of the police, unlike other public services, is that they just don't have to listen.

There is indeed a strong feeling and there is indeed displeasure; this can be described as anger, quite rightly. The difference is that the anger is not about pay, it is about civic responsibility, morality. Public service. There is a real danger that if this message continues to be lost, to be spun; the sense of duty behind it will be buried forever.

As a final thought, if you offered me the right to strike; I for one would tell you to keep it. I know I am not alone. The perception of the anger needs to change and the truth about this anger must be made clear to all. The truth of it is exactly what I've just shown you, in the words of serving officers and, some members of the public too.

The question is, as ever, are people willing to listen?

The Definition of a PCC:

"This did not bode well"

6th and 7th of July 2012

What follows is three parts of a two way conversation. Some will have seen this, some won't. I'm not going to comment any further on it, just make sure that both sides are relayed, exactly as they were.

****

I spoke to a PCC Candidate tonight, Mervyn Barrett of Lincolnshire. He has an OBE but is modest about it.

It started as the usual banter (it's actually quite fun with many PCC candidates) but then he began to refuse to answer questions from members of the public who were talking to him. This did not bode well. No room for dipping questions in policing.

He then went on to ignore questions from police officers about what genuine, operational reform was needed; after some initial rhetoric about wanting to talk.

Then something horrible happened. He defined himself. I know this sounds like it should be an involuntary bowel movement and, in truth, it is of sorts. He tweeted:
  "We must relentlessly push for efficiency and

look to partnerships with third and private sector if we are to improve standards and cut crime".

You need look no further back in this blog than The Slip of The Mask for my interpretation of PCC's to know this was inevitable. You also, all know my concerns over privatisation. Quite rightly Barrett was taken up on this, with people correctly stating that they had not yet heard anyone define what reform was, beyond pay.

Having heard this buzzword tripe often enough for my eyes to involuntarily roll back in my head, I pitched in with:
   "they don't know because they believe, genuinely believe, for us this is all about pay". (I had covered this in a blog and tweets only hours earlier after all)

Causing no surprise whatsoever Barrett replied:
   "what about your pension....*sarcastic grin*"

I picked this up a few tweets later and gave a straight reply:
   "Oh Mervyn. What about my pension exactly? Be frank, say what you mean. Come along. Be a brave little soldier".

This was after all a grown man talking like a toddler, so there was only one way to respond: adapt communication to your target audience.

And here is how Mervyn defined (or if you prefer, soiled) himself. By deleting the tweet. Then ignoring numerous requests to clarify why he had deleted it. He is not the brave little soldier I had hoped for.

Well, my concern is not for a flippant comment about my pension. I can cope with buffoons quite well. I'm not even bothered that he showed his true colours, by deviating from spin and into an insult. I expect that from politicians and find it fairly amusing. Back to toddlers, it's like the jokes my three year old tells. Funny because they mean nothing.

My concern is that there are over a million people that live in Lincolnshire and that, if elected, this man will be responsible for their safety, for the way in which they are policed. If he is willing to make a trivial comment then delete it, deny it and refuse to respond to a challenge on it...what on earth will he do with major issues affecting the people of Lincolnshire? What will happen to the promises he makes or, if he makes a mistake? Will that be buried? Will it be denied? Will it be ignored?

The problem with policing, that amateur, nose honking, clowns like this don't seem to understand is:
That there is no room for this kind of behaviour. No room for denial, for ignoring the difficult questions; no room for cowardice. The public deserve better.

If he is prepared to do this, at such a low level, before election, when he only has votes to lose...what will he be prepared to do on issues that could impact upon his career? For the people of Lincolnshire that's a terrifying thought and one, potentially, that will echo throughout the country for years to come. Let's not forget, Nick Herbert has made clear he wants PCCs to be set up in a way that makes it virtually impossible for any other party to undo them.

I had a quick look at Mervyn's site, his claims. 30 years in the field of crime reduction. 30 years writing papers and training the police. Astounding. Astounding when you realise he's spent 30 years trying to come up with ways to reduce re-offending and so forth. Astounding because, from an operational point of view, I can tell you it hasn't worked.

In fact it's pretty well established that re-offending has remained static at best or increased over the last 30 years. The crux of this being: if in 30 years you achieve limited impact in your own field of expertise, you don't stand much chance in someone else's and; should be careful about the things you say. Especially if you are not prepared to stand by them.

You know me I reflect upon things, so I thought I'd have a little look at this Barrett chap. In brief it rolls like this:

He got his OBE in 1999 for services to the National Association for the Care and Resettlement of Offenders (NACRO as we know it): (**24**). They seem to be pushing it as a crime prevention charity these days, rather than working with previous offenders.

This is his role within the organisation 'Head of Resettlement Information' (**25**). In an interview in September 2011 his focus appeared to be on exclusively on working with offenders (**26**). On the NACRO web site, if you were to access their 'Strategic Plan for 2011 - 2015', you'd get about as far as page 2 before you started to think 'agendas here'.

The foreword from the chair of trustees states "In this difficult period, we must step up our efforts to re-establish ourselves as the partner of choice for the rehabilitation agenda and as the voice of sense in the criminal justice debate".

There is lots of other stuff, literally lots but page 10 jumped out – strengths:
The last one says - "Through the Department for Work and Pensions' Work Programme we already have experience of operating in a payment-by-results culture."

Oh dear. Payment by results. Efficiency. Tripe. Let's not forget, Lincolnshire is already G4S country.

Finally, at the top of page 11, Opportunities - Market Development:
   "Bidding in partnership with like-minded organisations for offender management opportunities".
Again, isn't that what the Police do now, offender management? I believe the current fashion is to call it Integrated Offender Management (IOM for short). And...isn't that one of the sections highlighted as being 'outsourced' under the Police 'privatisation' agreements (or, let's get down with the OBEs

and call it business partnering).

I had a little look at NACRO and found that a former trustee Sir Graham Melmoth also sits with the Charities Aid Foundation, along with the likes of Gary Hoffman of Barclays. For those of you that don't know the Charities Aid Foundation (and this is merely a little sideline now) it is described by Powerbase as follows:

"The Charities Aid Foundation (CAF) "puts donors in control of their giving, and helps charities make the most of what they get." But one look at the headings on their website (**27**) and you might start to think that you would be better off with a political lobbyist:
Change the world today - We can help you make a little gift go a long way; Take control of your giving; Engage your employees; Make more of your money — With our award-winning charity financial services; Bank with us; Investigate investments; Informing big decisions — From government to grass roots Our research; Influencing policy

There is a feel of 'millionaires only' with its statements such as:
"If you have more than $10m (£5m) to give to charity, we can help you to register your own independent charitable foundation, regardless

of your nationality.""'

A bit more influence, just what the world needs. They are professionally advised by Deloitte...you know the ones who sponsored the Policy Exchange event on PCCs. Just another little piece of the big old web.

NACRO is also linked to the New Deal Task force by Helen Edwards who was or is Chief Executive of NACRO. (I'm not interested enough to check which at the moment).

NDTF changed its name to the National Employment panel in 2001. Again there are a few bankers sat in there. Chair of the Prudential, that kind of thing. The NET had a board made up of numerous people and included high rankers from big consultancies like KPMG, Accenture and so forth. If you want to look up more, it'll be DIY.

I'd like to conclude by simply saying I've never liked cowards and; all the cowards I've met have the massive propensity to be liars. Liars and cowards should not be entrusted with the public safety of over a million people. That is my opinion. I said it and, unlike some; I'm standing by it.

****

This morning I received the following from Mervyn Barrett in response to the blog:

"@MervynBarrett: @J_amesp Hi, could you DM me your best contact details please - email etc. Many thanks, Mervyn"

Taking into consideration his failure to engage openly or repeat his initial comment I am not convinced his motive is to talk through the issues.

Subsequently I have posted two immediate replies:

"@J_amesp: @MervynBarrett on two conditions
1) explain your pensions comment in open forum and 2) explain why you want my contact details in open forum"

and;

"@J_amesp: @MervynBarrett I am also happy to host a   reply and your feelings to the blog, or post an update   incorporating your views. More than happy."

As yet I have received no reply. Once I do I will happily take an appropriate course of action. I make clear, I am more than happy to have my opinion changed and if he makes his wishes or thoughts crystalline: I will either post an updated blog with his side of the story or write a new blog incorporating both.

I believe this kind of discussion is exactly what open debate forums are for. Once again, I am happy to do what is necessary to draw a satisfactory conclusion for us both. That's the best way to end any discussion.

****

I am very pleased to publish the response from Mervyn Barrett, PCC candidate for Lincolnshire. I win five pounds in a bet with myself that a certain 'L' word would be used by the end of it.

"I believe that police reform is long overdue. While crime has fallen substantially over the past 15 years, much of that reduction has been due to a strong economy rather than improved police performance. Despite a significant real terms increase in funding in recent years, detection rates have not significantly improved, with only a quarter of crimes being 'cleared up'. A third of the public who come in contact with the police are dissatisfied with the response they receive and most of those who complain are unhappy with the way the police deal with their complaint.

The Policing Minister has said that the police are the poorest performers of the public services. That said, I know from past experience that there are vast numbers of police officers who see their roles as a vocation and work beyond their remits in order to do a good, conscientious job.

I want to see such officers properly rewarded, which is why I support Tom Winsor's reforms and believe that he is the right man to be Chief Inspector of Constabulary. The reforms are designed to reward the best officers as well as facilitating the introduction and use of modern management practices in the police in line with practices elsewhere in the public sector and the wider economy. I am standing as Police and Crime Commissioner because I know about crime and policing.

I have helped lead an organisation that has more than 40 years' experience of working with the police and other professionals, both to prevent crime in local communities and to stop offenders from re-offending - and I myself have over thirty years experience in the field. Fewer offenders means fewer victims of crime. At the heart of my past work in run-down neighbourhoods has been consultation. We have consulted local people about the problems they experience and the solutions to those problems. Often the solutions lie with local communities.

I am standing as an Independent. I have never been a member of a political party. I believe that the public should expect more of their Commissioner than they are likely to get from any party political party candidate. I believe that people should expect more from their police, and expect more from the criminal justice system which too often has let them down.

I am standing for Commissioner because I care about reducing crime and offending and my focus will be on one thing: what works in reducing crime and the fear of crime. I am surprised by the tone of the recent criticism of me. I do not think I have ever been called a liar or coward before and am somewhat hurt by this libel, which I strongly suggest is not repeated."

I am sorely disappointed in the lack of real content, considering the over 24 hour response time and, the fact this has clearly been put together with the assistance of a team. Most particularly I am disappointed in the fact that the issue of the deleted tweet remains not only unresolved but; unmentioned. Therefore, the courage necessary to keep the public safe on much more difficult topics remains, in my eyes, in grave doubt.

I have made my feelings quite clear on the broader implication of this deleted tweet and do not need to repeat them here. My opinion remains unchanged.

As for those who read this; I know you are more than capable of forming your own judgements.

I had hoped for better. I had hoped for the start of meaningful debate arising out of humility. I had hoped for an apology and the firm virtual handshake that would have come with. There is none forthcoming and my questions remain unanswered but, there was the response nonetheless. I would like to thank Mervyn (and his team*) for coming up with this reply. I am wholly satisfied with it. Wholly.

---

*On Sunday the 21st of October 2012, the day of publication of this second edition, *The Telegraph* printed an article by Andrew Gilligan with the following heading:
   "A high-profile candidate campaigning to become one of the Government's new elected Police and Crime Commissioners is being secretly backed by American neo-conservative lobbyists and companies pushing for police privatisation". The article related to Mervyn Barrett.

The Value of Goodwill:

"fanciful things, plucked out of the air, to suit
ideology rather than reality"

7th of July 2012

I've often pondered if you can put a monetary value on good will.

I was not entirely sure that it was possible, not least of all within the police service. Thousands of officers, work thousands of hours a year, that they don't claim for. I know, I'm one of them. I do it because I love what I do; and because I care about putting the time in, to do it right.

This can even mean the little things, like being at your station half an hour before your shift, getting kitted up, checking emails, booking on, checking crimes and intelligence. Checking the files in your rack or docket. Getting an update, about what incidents are ongoing, from the team you are relieving. Slowly this particular element of good will is eroding, because officers have had enough. They are worn out by shift changes, to cover shortfalls; sick of being treated 'like dogs' as many would say. It's sad.

You may think that officers should simply go on duty, officially, the half hour earlier; from experience I can tell you, much fuss will be made and, many nasty things said. The same applies if you were to to turn up on time and then do all of this before going to briefing. In a bizarre twist, this good will has become enforced. It's worth noting, that in Germany some years ago, a police force was taken to court for the fifteen minutes 'kit up' time and; the officers won. The force had to back date pay and time off. This is what originally got me thinking...I supposed on hearing this that it IS possible, to put a value on good will; if you have to.

So what if you are under no obligation?

You'd have to work through this logically of course, starting with the consideration at the other end of a shift, which is covered clearly in the police regulations (covering pay and conditions).

Essentially if you work half an hour over your 'rostered' shift, it is for free, for the first four occasions within that 'working week'; i.e. that group of six shifts in a row. This is widely known as the 'Queen's Half Hour'. Time that was 'bought out' some years ago. I chuckle at the thought of buying good will but, in all seriousness, it appears that buying it out has seen an end to proper recording of it.

As the 'Queen's Half Hour' is in play in impromptu or unplanned overtime, it is referred to as Casual Overtime. For my liking that has always sounded a little nonchalant; I'd rarely describe anything relating to public safety as casual. Can you imagine the number of intelligence reports that get put on in this half an hour? That could potentially save a life while the officers go home to rest? Public safety is, let's not forget, the first duty of a police officer.

There is also a duty, in law, for all police forces to record the working hours of officers and, to keep detailed financial records too; this is a public service, paid for by the public, after all. This information, as a simple number of hours and subsequently 'unpaid pay', should be quite simple to calculate. Shouldn't it? Well, no. That is the answer.

Out of 43 Forces in England and Wales, that received FOI requests, 'meaningful' responses were only received from 16. I think we should do 'stats', it's a fashion thing, so let's say that 62.7% of forces didn't answer in meaningful way.

7 Forces issued an outright refusal notice to provide the information, every single one based on the cost of supplying the information from manual records. So, 16.2% of forces refused to provide the information for financial reasons.

1 of those 7 has rejected an appeal for at least some information. So, 14% of forces refusing to provide the information, also refused appeals.

7 Forces have provided partial information sufficient to form an estimation of the value. So, 16.2% of forces have provided some information.

2 Forces (Sussex and City of London) provided a comprehensive answer. So, finally, only 4.6% of forces provided a comprehensive reply.

Based on the full and partial (so fundamentally incomplete) information, supplied by the 9 Forces, the nearest estimated value of the Queen's Half Hour, unpaid Casual Overtime, for 2011/12 is £323,686.

Over 42 forces (Metropolitan Police Service excluded) this gives a baseline estimate of over £1.5 million pounds, in the last year alone. This is without going in depth on the varying hourly rates, that come with the pay scales and ranks. This tells me three things:

1) That working time and financial recording in police forces, up and down the country, is woeful.

2) The good will at the start of the shifts is worth at least a further £1.5 million annually, making a 'best minimum guess' value of £3 million a year. Yes, as a bare minimum, good will is worth £3 million a year. (or a minimum of £30 million every ten years. Or a minimum of £90 million, since the much trumpeted pay reform over thirty years ago. It's worth noting that, even thirty years of good will is ten million short of paying for the increasingly farcical PCC fiasco.

And;

3) There is no way on God's green earth that I, nor anyone else, can trust any reform agenda that makes a big song and dance about 80% of police cost being manpower; when the true value of that can't even be recorded, or quantified properly.

In fact I'd go as far as saying that this little nugget, on its own, throws the whole cuts and reform calculation into doubt....because what is it based on? As I've long suspected; it's based upon fanciful things, plucked out of the air, to suit ideology rather than reality.

If the police forces themselves don't know what their biggest expense is actually costing them, or giving to them (therefore being profit), then: the Home Office, slashing away like the grim reaper on Crystal Meth, will have no idea whatsoever.

I've excluded the Met simply because Twitter says that there are between 250,000 and 500,000 cancelled rest days for officers to be resolved, from the last 12 months. I don't want to try and put a value on that, until its been confirmed as true by either the Federation or other means; you know me. I'm nothing if not fair.

This further trip to big top, the land of big shoes, where noses are honked ad infinitum, also says quite a lot about the frankly boring Clock in/Clock out arguments being spun...by people who had fundamentally written the Winsor Report in 2007 (*in the original blog post this read 2005, which referred to the period before the 2006 and David Cameron speech. Here it is changed to 2007 to reflect the publication of the interim report produced on the issue)*. Don't worry, I'll get to that soon.

For now, with good will to the tune of at least £3 million, in the last twelve months alone; I bid you adieu.

Fifty Shades of Outsourcing:

"the suit watched in ever unfolding horror as the office of constable rose"

8th of July 2012

In the dark room with the gritty floor, the empty pot of lubricant lay, gathering dust in the corner; a distant memory.

The chains rattled in the darkness, ever more softly as the fight began to falter; the weight of continued pressure and abuse, of tricks and ploys, of being treated like a dog, finally making resistance almost impossible.

Almost.

The Office of Constable lay prostrate and shackled as, at the top of the basement stairs, a group in suits slowly opened the door...

I'll come back to this.

I've been told two more stories this week, about G4S. I'm not going to relay them with any comment from me, just as they were told. I trust the people telling me this but I make clear, this is their word; all I am doing I relaying it because I feel it is worth sharing. As ever I welcome comment, response and debate.

A colleague working with a constabulary, that is now partnered in a ten year deal with G4S, had this to say:

"Life working with G4S hasn't really started to bite yet - though the sight of "those" logos on the shoulders of former Police Staff colleagues does take some getting used to. (**28, 29** & **30**). The basic effect is on morale and motivation of many of those colleagues who were transferred across, often against their wishes.

"You still have a job!" is the underlining message. The fact is that the staff have chosen to work for the Police and therefore for the Public. (**31**).

They know that the business bottom-line is coming into play, and that all activity is costed. "Saving jobs" has now transformed, within a very short space of time, into up to 60 job losses. (**32**)

Note who gets the blame:
    Lincolnshire Police have asked for further efficiency measures."

And, further south, the picture really is no prettier. Please note this is from the horse's mouth and, you are unlikely to find it in any newspapers:

"I, with many others, have received my training for delivery of security at the Olympic

Park. It was a chaotic shambles to say the least. We are so close now and yet still don't know which teams we will be allocated to. The largest entrance point, 120 search lanes, has now been handed over to the army, so G4S will mainly be focusing on perimeter security at the 137 venues and, operating the rest of the search lanes.

Each venue has 100 staff allocated with a 15% built in allowance for daily drop outs.

We have been explicitly told however, that we should expect up to 40% of staff not to show up daily. This is clearly dangerous and there is no further resilience, of any real description, built into this. It raises serious questions as to whether security will be compromised.

How could it not be? You don't need to look much further back than the search dog stories in the paper (**33**) to realise this is not the professional operation it's been branded as. It's terrifying; the staff on duty records were clearly doctored to avoid fines....fines arising from missed targets! Where are the ethics? The G4S definition of accountability is not mine.

The search lanes are a worry too. They've set targets to process 350 ticket holders per hour.

What do you think matters more here? Meeting targets or safety?

Each lane takes 8-10 staff to operate and if the X-Ray operator is off (not all are trained) I think they'll keep the lane open anyway to meet the target. That's just a gut feeling and, if the predicted drop out rate of 40% is replicated, I can see no other way they could do it. What's terrifying is that soon, this will be replicated in police forces across the country. Targets first, public safety second".

Food for thought for you today. Thought food for me too. So, with that, back to the beginning...

...the stairs creaked as suit after suit walked slowly down them; their ghostly, sarcastic and eager grins floating in the light from the open door.

Down on the floor the Office of Constable relaxed, hands and feet unbound, shackles hanging open and loosely around them. Just enough of an illusion in the dark. A deep breath, the spare handcuff key protruding from between bruised and bloodied knuckles. Dust and grit shook to the floor, as the first suit, reached the last step. The grin faltered as they were pushed forwards by the now excited and aroused suit behind them.

In the dark, confined space, with little room for manoeuvre, the suit watched in ever unfolding horror as the Office of Constable rose. Smiling and stepped softly forwards; speaking in barely a whisper.

"The truth of this is, I'm not trapped down here with you any more...". Advancing one further step, feet also whispering, in the grit. "The truth is, you're trapped down here with me".

The History of the Future:

"there is a significant amount of correspondence that 'senior colleagues' do not want in the public domain"

8th of July 2012

Ever since I joined the police a Shakespeare quote has always stayed at the forefront of my mind:

"How far that little candle throws his beams! So shines a good deed in a naughty world."

Over the past few months that has almost become my mantra. It certainly seems appropriate; as I've increasingly discovered, there is a lot out there that could do with some good light upon it. Also, I would much prefer to live my life knowing that I was brave enough to take a look. To say what I saw. It can be daunting, scary even, not just throwing those flickering beams out there, not just finding unpleasant things crawling and slithering in the dark; but also doing so, knowing that 'people have long memories'. That's a phrase many coppers will know. It's a phrase I really don't think needs any explanation.

It's funny, some people have called me fearless some have called me courageous. I don't think of myself like that at all. I have a healthy respect of fear, it's kept my instincts alive and, kept me in one piece, more than a few times. The best way I can explain how I see it, is in the words of another literary great, Mark Twain:

"Courage is resistance to fear, mastery of fear, not absence of fear".

I keep my fear on a leash, under control and that allows me to do what I do.

I've been looking into today's topic for a while now and it's been a big task, trying to put it into context but I think, I hope, this will do it justice.
I've said before that this reform agenda was pre-planned, I had a gut feeling from the outset. So, I've shone my little beam and seen what I've seen.

It appears that the truth in this particular shadow is quite clear.

What's happening now, this reform of the service I love, the future of political interference and vested interests, of profit over public duty; has feet firmly planted in the past. It is hard to fill the gaps in completely, as much is left publicly unsaid. Hard but...it is possible.

The final key to the link between the future and the past came via an FOI request, lodged by a person who I can never thank; I have no idea who they are.

On the 4th of April they wrote to the Home Office asking for "all relevant information (recorded and in any other form) as regards to what remit or briefing was given to Tom Winsor, with regards to his review of police officer and staff pay and conditions and what the desired outcome was".

On the 3rd of May 2012 the request was effectively dismissed with this reply from the Home Office:
    "Your letter requests details of 'all relevant information (recorded and in any other form) as regards to what remit or briefing was given to Tom Winsor, with regards to his review of police officer and staff pay and conditions and what the desired outcome was.'

The terms of reference for the review are a public document and can be accessed at (**34**) I also enclose a letter sent to Tom Winsor on 6 May 2011 about the scope
and timing of the part 2 report in relation to police pensions' issues".

The website is informative and, for me, the key phrase in the Terms of Reference is this:
    "enable modern management practices in line with practices elsewhere in the public sector

and the wider economy"

This, to me, says: make sure there is a way for lean management practices to be applied, which includes budget based workforce reductions, allow for third party Police and Crime Commissioners to be able to make changes too and allow for the private sector to make a move into policing. Also, to allow all of that to work, introduce compulsory redundancy for people with no right to strike. Maybe that's just me.

On the 4th of May, the same FOI user sent this request to the Home Office:
   "can you please supply me with all documentation exchanged between the Home Secretary or any other officials within the Home Office and Tom Winsor, recorded in hand-written copy, email, minutes of meetings, letters, notes and any other form of documentation either in hard copy or electronic form. This documentation should cover all correspondence between the Home Office and Tom Winsor between the dates of 1st August, 2010 and 1st March 2012."

Clearly this would have produced a substantial amount of correspondence, given the topic and should have been easy to produce, as Tom Winsor had a small and dedicated support team, working with him, at the Home Office. It's here that things start to get interesting.

On the 6th of June 2012 the Home Office gave an initial reply:

"I regret we are unable to send you a full response to your request within 20 working days, as required by the Act. This is because consultation is still on going with a number of senior colleagues."

I would love to have been a fly on the wall at these senior consultations. How senior were they? What exactly was the issue?

Eventually, 23 days later, on the 29th of June 2012, following this senior level consultation on the release of correspondence for 349 days of detailed work, the Home Office released five...yes five...emails:

"Email from Tom Winsor to Stephen Kershaw, Andrew Wren and Stephen Rimmer dated 18 March 2011, forwarding an email he had sent to forces about the Part 1 report. Three emails between Tom Winsor and Stephen Kershaw dated 22 February and 24 February 2012 about restricted duty and the timings for the Final report. One e-mail from Tom Winsor dated 25 January 2012 regarding progress of Part 2 of the Police pay review."

Believe it or not, I don't deduce from this that there were five emails alone, during this whole period, neither that there was no written correspondence; nor indeed, that there was no correspondence at all between March 2011 and January 2012.

I am a reasonable man and, from this, I reasonably suspect two things. That there is a significant amount of correspondence that 'senior colleagues' do not want in the public domain. And; that there is no coincidence that this reply came three days after the pre-appointment hearing at the HASC; at which Tom Winsor and Crime and Justice Minister, Nick Herbert, appeared.

In fact, in respect of point one, I actually know that there is a large amount of correspondence, and that is held on Home Office systems. I know this because it's written in the Home Office reply, the same reply in which they released only five emails. Their exact words were these:

"During the review Tom Winsor received administrative and other assistance from a small support team comprised of Home Office officials who worked directly for him and under his instruction. We are aware there was a large amount of written communication between

Tom Winsor and this support team in the course of the review. These communications are stored on Home Office systems and the content is information held by the Home Office for the purposes of the FOIA."

They claimed it would have cost more than £600 to provide more information. Really? Here's a five second conversation (and yes, I timed it):

"Hi, can you print your emails from the last twelve months or so, from when you've been on Tom Winsor's support team. Thanks."

Say we repeat this ten times, that's fifty seconds. Now be patient with this next bit, I am after all a two fingered typist...Say each has 200 emails (2000 in total), neatly and efficiently saved in sub folders as any good professional would, click the folder, hit CTRL+A then hit CTRL+P. The emails then queue and print and they carry on about their business without further need for intervention.

Say we do this ten times, the actual process takes around fifteen seconds before the machine takes over; that's one minute and thirty seconds. Anyway, that's two minutes and twenty seconds...you see where I'm going. For under £600 I'd have expected significantly more than five random emails. This leads my sense of quite reasonable suspicion back to the second half of point one; senior colleagues.

There is little of interest within the five released emails, that is until you read this one:

"From: Winsor, Tom
Sent: 22 February 2012 11:57
To: Kershaw Stephen
Subject: Restricted duty
Importance: High
Sensitivity: Confidential

Stephen

I attach a draft legal definition of 'restricted duty' and I'd greatly appreciate your thoughts.
Is this on target?
I've also sent it to [REDACTED].

Best regards
Tom"

I read it once and thought 'on target' meant date. Then I read it again. It doesn't mean date, not at all. He's referring to the legal definition being on target. What target?

Why is an Independent Reviewer asking the Home Office if his legal definition, for something within his own review, yet to be presented to the Home Office, is on target? Why does he need their thoughts? The reply, two days later, is no less concerning:

"From: Kershaw Stephen
Sent: Friday, February 24, 2012 08:09 PM
To: Winsor, Tom
Subject: FW: Restricted duty

Tom

Many thanks. [REDACTED] has let you have some comments which incorporated. reactions from my folk, and I don't think that we have anything more to add. How is 15 March looking now for ETA on Winsor 2, pse?

SEK"

I'm hugely curious to know who [REDACTED] is, they must have real issues with all sorts of day to activity if their name can't be said. Also, I wonder what the 'folk' had to add to Mr Winsor's independently written legal definition, to go into his final independent report, days before the proposed release.

This isn't a criticism of Mr Winsor. By all accounts he is thoroughly pleasant fellow, though often described as naive. Without the full correspondence being published, I can do nothing but continue to suspect that the report was actually written to a set of targets, much more specific than those given in the terms of reference. I am after all a police officer and gaps in information like this need investigating; especially when that little alarm bell is ringing.

I pondered this information gap. Who [REDACTED] could be and, what kind of targets could possibly have been in existence? As you know of me by now, I've found out quite a lot, about a lot of interlinked topics, about individuals, in a short space of time. So I focused. I began looking back and found something I had seen before but not really paid too much attention to, at the time. I know someone else's alarm bell was ringing too as they also sent it to me, out of the blue.

The document I'm referring to can be found, in full, here: (35). It's the April 2007 Mid Term Report from the Conservative Police Reform Task Force. It was written, over five years ago, by Nick Herbert, with the help of Oscar Keeble, Aidan Burley and Blair Gibbs; it also gives helpful little biographies for each of them.

"Nick Herbert was elected Conservative MP for Arundel & South Downs in May 2005 and appointed Shadow Minister for Police Reform later that year. Prior to his election he was Director of Reform, the independent think tank which he co-founded in 2002. He was previously Chief Executive of Business for Sterling,where he launched the successful 'no' campaign against the Euro, and Director of Political Affairs for the British Field Sports Society. He played a leading role in setting up the Countryside Movement, which became the Countryside Alliance."

Of course we know that Mr Herbert is now the Crime and Justice Minister.

"Oscar Keeble is a political researcher who has worked with Nick Herbert on police reform since September 2006. He graduated from the London School of Economics with an honours degree in Government and studied for a Masters in International Political Economy at the Politics and International Studies Department of the University of Warwick, where he was awarded a distinction and achieved the highest grade in his year. He has also worked at the think tank Reform."

Keeble appears to have been a Senior Consultant at Deloitte (sponsors and speakers at the Policy Exchange PCC event) and is now based is Switzerland as an Economic Affairs Officer at the UN.

"Aidan Burley is a management consultant at Hedra Plc5 who has been seconded to the office of Nick Herbert MP since January 2007. He specialises in criminal justice and welfare reform, strategic change and performance improvement. He has spent much of the past five years working on projects to improve the performance of the police and wider criminal justice system. His previous clients have included the Cabinet Office, Home Office, Metropolitan Police Service, Hampshire Police and Nottinghamshire Police. He graduated from St John's College, Oxford and is an elected Conservative Councillor in Hammersmith & Fulham."

Burley is now the Conservative MP for Cannock Chase.

"Blair Gibbs is Campaign Director of the Tax Payers' Alliance which monitors value for money in public services and argues for lower taxes and greater accountability. He graduated from Merton College, Oxford before joining the think tank Reform in 2005, where he was the Home Affairs researcher specialising in accountability, prisons policy and neighbourhood policing. He co-authored the Reform report Urban Crime Rankings (July 2006) which made the first systematic attempt to rank cities and towns on per capita recorded crime to advance the argument for better local information on crime rates. He has contributed to this report in a personal capacity."

Gibbs, as we know, went to be Nick Herbert's Staff Officer, before becoming head of Crime and Justice at the Policy Exchange. He is rumoured to be heading to City Hall in a police advisory role.

Other thanks went to:

Ben Wallace – MP for Wyre and Preston North.
Barry Loveday – Appears to be a Reader in Criminal Justice Administration based at Portsmouth University.
Gordon Wasserman – Conservative Lord, advisor on Policing and Criminal Justice.
And;
Alex Chalk – Appears to be a Barrister and Conservative Councillor at Hammersmith and Fulham.

The central premise of the report was that, "in spite of record spending on law and order, crime remains far too high. A more effective criminal justice system and social action will be important components of a new approach to fighting crime. But the police are a vital link in the chain of justice, consuming two-thirds of law and order spending. Their performance over the next decade will be essential in improving the quality of life of millions of citizens."

It goes on to say:
"The closure of police stations is emblematic of the withdrawal of the police from the public. On paper, police officer numbers have increased – the police workforce has grown by almost 25 percent in the last five years. In practice, the public simply do not see it...If the amount of time a police officer spends on the beat could be increased from one fifth to two fifths, this would effectively double the police presence on the streets of England and Wales without recruiting a single additional officer."

Possibly the most bizarre thing in the foreword, considering the ongoing revelations of thousands of officers being cut from forces, by the now established government is this:
"When more police were put on the streets of

central London after 7/7, crime fell".

And this:

"To meet these challenges it will be vital to ensure that the police are properly resourced in the future."

This is almost as startlingly obvious as the news in The Guardian this month, that long prison sentences reduce re-offending. Herbert et al conclude the foreword with these recommendations:

"The structure of the police must enable them to fight serious crime while enhancing and sustaining community policing. This means either the existing 43 forces co-operating much more effectively, or a new national force taking responsibility for serious crime while much more localised forces focus on volume crime in their areas."

We now have the NCA (*National Crime Agency*).

"The complexity and demands of modern policing mean that the workforce must be reformed to ensure that it is flexible, well trained and highly motivated, with a diverse range of skills and expertise. A key goal should be to enhance the ability of police chiefs to manage their workforces."

Here is a large part of the Winsor Part 1 and Part 2 reports in a nutshell, years before it was written.

"The police's hands must be untied to give them the discretion they need and to release officers for front-line duties. Central direction and targets should be replaced by locally accountable leadership and priority setting. Civilian staff or the private sector should be employed to do jobs which sworn officers do not need to do, and the police 'family' should be extended."

Here are PCCs and Privatisation; long before they became real.

In a very forward thinking, face-palm, Chapter 1 opens with this statement:
"Crime is high by international and historical standards. The Government's claims to have reduced crime are not borne out by reality...The Government claims that crime measured by the British Crime Survey has fallen, yet the British Crime Survey massively underestimates crime. It covers only half of recorded crime and ignores murder, rape, fraud, crimes against under-16s, commercial crime including

shoplifting, and crime where there is no direct victim such as drugs dealing. Estimates suggest the true figure of crime in England and Wales is roughly three times the level indicated by the British Crime Survey."

Lets not forget the number of times in recent months (and weeks) that we've heard quotes about crime falling to justify police cuts. Its history repeating, just with the role reversed. Chapter 2 begins with this statement:

"As police stations have closed and foot patrol has given way to modern policing methods, the police have become increasingly alienated from the public. The way to rebuild public confidence and tackle crime is to have police officers on the streets."

As we all know, stations continue to close at an alarming rate and with thousands more officer roles to go, the likelihood of more feet on the street occurring in the real world is evaporating. In fact the report even says this:

"An increased police presence on the streets cuts crime. A study of the aftermath of 7/7, when increased police numbers on the streets in six London boroughs led to falls in crime, suggests that a 10 per cent increase in police deployment reduces the crime rate by approximately 3 percent."

Chapter 3 arrives and we start to get a real sense of the current direction:
"The police currently face five key challenges: terrorism, serious and organised crime, establishing community policing, strengthening local accountability, and delivering improved value for money. The police face several obstacles to meeting these challenges, including excessive bureaucracy and central intervention, an inflexible workforce, and inefficient procedures."

They then make four recommendations, two of which are again a firm part of the Winsor Reports:
"2 The police workforce must be reformed to ensure that it is flexible, well trained and highly motivated, with a diverse range of skills and expertise, and that forces provide value for money."
and;
"4 The police need to be made properly accountable for their performance as well as their conduct, and their performance management framework must only reward activity that delivers a better service, not activity which keeps officers busy and ticks boxes."

Chapter Five continues to outline the Winsor Report recommendations, years before it was written:

"If the police are to meet today's challenges they will require a workforce that is flexible, highly skilled, well motivated, fairly paid and representative of the population it serves. Workforce reform, a new focus on training and leadership, easier entry for talented individuals, and greater flexibility for police managers will form a key part of the new police agenda."

It goes on:

"The Treasury estimates that £250 million could be saved through better overtime and sick pay management. Flexibility may be increased by reducing overtime payments and paying officers a higher basic salary in return, although any changes to overtime must be evaluated in terms of operational effectiveness and recruitment and retention, as well as efficiency. Pay should reflect skills as well as seniority. The police pension scheme should allow people to leave and join the force at the right time. While the vast majority of police officers are well motivated professionals working to high standards, it is too difficult to remove bad, unmotivated, and even corrupt police officers. It is essential that the mechanism for disciplining officers is proportionate, timely, transparent, fair and cost-effective. Recent changes have simplified the process of removing bad officers. If, after these changes have bedded in, the mechanism still does not achieve these goals, further reform will be necessary."

Or if you prefer, Winsor Part 2.

Recommendations 46 and 47 will allow for a compulsory severance (redundancy) scheme for police officers. Recommendations 53 to 74 deal with pay scales.
"The maximum basic pay for constables will remain at £36,519. The number of pay scales will be reduced from 10 to 7. Pay scales 6, 7 and 9 will be removed. At pay point 4 Constables will also be required to pass a "Foundation Skills Threshold" test before progression. This test will also be subject to retests every 5 years. Any officer who fails this test will be subject to UPP (Unsatisfactory Performance Procedures)".

Herbert's report continues:
"The complexity and demands of modern policing have created a greater need for graduate recruits to the police. However, studies show that only 10-16 per cent of police recruits are graduates. The High Potential

Development Scheme is currently under review but its replacement must ensure that more graduates are recruited. There is also a strong case for encouraging talented managers and professionals from outside the police force to enter at a rank above constable."

Or, if you prefer, Winsor Part 2.

Recommendations 8 and 19 suggest that direct entry schemes should be set up for the appointment of Inspectors and Superintendents.

"Recommendations 23 to 26 will allow for a Chief Constable to be appointed from a police force outside of the United Kingdom – Another direct entry route!

Recommendation 30 allows for rank skipping so that an officer won't have to serve in every rank as they progress through their career".

Herbert's report goes on to say:

"More than 8,000 officers are being paid a full-time salary while on restricted duties. The wage bill of these officers, who account for almost 6 per cent of the total police workforce, is £243 million a year. Sick pay and restricted duties must be better managed. Similarly, injury pensions must be fair and proportionate."

Or if your prefer, Winsor Part 2.

Recommendation 39:

"If an officer is on restricted duties for one year their pay will be reduced by £2,922 per annum. If they then continue on restricted duties for another year proceedings should be commenced to either dismiss or ill-health retire them."

Chapter 7 covers PCCs with no real surprises but then, we reach the big finish:

"Her Majesty's Inspectorate of Constabulary is too close to the Government and police forces. There needs to be a more independent and rigorous inspectorate that will serve as champion of the people rather than the police."

I am fairly sure this was the exact wording used in the speeches, following the announcement of Tom Winsor as the new HMIC. In fact, it even goes on to say this, which I know I've heard very recently:

"It should report to Parliament rather than the Home Office and inspectors should be appointed by Parliament, not the Home Secretary. It should become in part an economic regulator, ensuring value for money as well as monitoring standards."

The history of the future, a future close at hand now, is quite clear. Everything I've heard and seen in the last couple of years...everything that has been branded as part of an independent review process, was preordained, almost word for word, by the people now churning it out; spinning their socks off.

I hope they can spin the fact they could see the future, including the contents and recommendations of an independent report; years before pen was put to paper. It seems that the legal definition of restricted duties was on target. It seems that quite a lot was on target, just on the basis of what I've read again. Perhaps the only way for this to be resolved is for the Home Office to release all of the correspondence, into the public domain. Perhaps those same senior colleagues should consider this, so that quite reasonable suspicion, that all is not well, can be alleviated.

And so, I move my little candle beam away and leave this in the light for you to digest. I hope this deed shines; in this clearly, very naughty world.

The Sound of Panic:

"the information, if released, would cause such havoc that the Home Office would grind to a halt"

9th of July 2012

What does panic sound like? How can you pick up on it, amongst a lot of other background noise? It's easy really. First you just need to establish what induces it.

In a criminal, it could be impending capture. In a ship's crew, it could be the approaching iceberg. In the case of the Home Office, it seems to be a relatively straight forward question.

The question was this:
   "In relation to Tom Winsor's selection as Preferred Candidate for the post of Chief Inspector of Constabulary can you please supply me with all documentation exchanged between the Home Secretary and any other officials within the Home Office recorded in hand-written copy, email, minutes of meetings, letters, notes and any other form of documentation either in hard copy or electronic form which relate to his selection for this post. This should specifically include minutes of all meetings held by the selection panel and any notes made by members of the selection panel. Could you also please supply me with the names of all persons who sat on the selection panel for this post."

I make clear, this question wasn't asked by me but primarily because I was beaten to it.

Panic, is an often overwhelming fear, often suffered by many people at once. Panic starts, as a murmur. Today, the response to that question, combined with the reply regarding the correspondence in my last blog, provides more than a murmur.

I can almost feel the tremor from here:
   "We are considering your request. Although the Act carries a presumption in favour of disclosure, it provides exemptions which may be used to withhold information in specified circumstances. Some of these exemptions, referred to as 'qualified exemptions', are subject to a public interest test. This test is used to balance the public interest in disclosure against the public interest in favour of withholding the information. The Act allows us to exceed the 20 working day response target where we need to consider the public interest test fully. The information you have requested is being considered under the exemption in section 36 of the Act, which relates to prejudice to the effective conduct of public affairs. This is a qualified exemption and to consider the public interest test fully we need to extend the 20 working day response period. We now aim

to let you have a full response by 6 August".

Anything to do with the police, how it is managed and reformed, is without a shadow of doubt in the public interest. I can't imagine why a single member of the public would not want to know this. To make sure it was being done properly, fairly; for the right reasons. The key here is this; "prejudice to the effective conduct of public affairs".

This tells me that the information, if released, would cause such havoc that the Home Office would grind to a halt, police reform would grind to a halt and that, potentially, 'senior colleagues' may have some real issues to deal with. Hell would freeze, the ice caps would melt, Towcester would be squashed by a giant marshmallow.

It would be bad, in short.

Of course, as no different answer is forthcoming, I am free to suspect reasonably and; to speculate as wildly as I see fit. I wonder; how quickly the reforms to FOI will come now? I wonder too, is there any coincidence, that this extended date ensures that the pension reform deadline is concluded by that point?

If I've learned anything about politics it's this: you become acceptably expendable, as long as the bill gets through, before your head rolls. I hear panic. I can feel it building. The Home Office are scared witless. It seems that the amount of things they are keeping out of the public domain increases daily; that they have an awful lot to hide. Of course, I'm entitled to think this and say it, because I have seen nothing to make me think otherwise. For today, I rest.

The Little Light in the Darkness:

"the risk to public safety, is little more than a business expansion opportunity"

10th of July 2012

I have sworn an oath.

It does not rest. It does not sleep. It takes more than it gives. It means, even on the days when a storm blows around us, we must carry on; even with heavy hearts and saddened souls. It means, we must keep our emotions in check, stay keen in our focus; even when the words of others, are a tinderbox in the hay barn. We have all been reminded, of the ultimate gravity, of that responsibility.

I intend to carry on; to do what needs to be done. I will keep my promise, even on the darkest of days. My candle will continue to cast it's light. Deep breath.

It's also quite an interesting profile of the man and, the company ambitions, laid out three years ago. This quote is by far the most telling:

"Mr Buckles believes G4S will benefit from the recession. "It helps our business in a number of ways," he says. "Criminality picks up during a recession, so yes we'll have a little bit of negativity around more robberies on our trucks. But on the other hand, there'll be a bigger increase in crime and more civil unrest so we'll get more business in that respect."

For me, this confirms everything I thought and, tells you everything you need to know about G4S; about the genuine mentality, at the top. The suffering of the public, during unprecedented world recession and, the risk to public safety, is little more than a business expansion opportunity. A way to enhance revenue streams. As a person, let alone police officer, this makes me shudder.

Buckles' job also appears to be 'relatively' well paid. In this article (**37**) from April this year, it's clearly laid out. He made £5.3 million in 2011 and that's with handing back a bonus, due to miring the company in a 'costly failed takeover bid'. It's a small wonder he looks so happy in the picture. His basic salary was £830,000 plus almost £30,000 in perks (car, insurance, etc).

His pension increased by £1.6 million, now giving him a pot of around £9 million. He also received shares totalling £2.9 million, with £1.1 million of them being backdated from 2008. He will be able to cash the stock in, in 2014, if he hits performance targets.

This is not a bad deal at all for the leader of a company, that is proving to have a concerning inability to staff the Olympic Park properly; or safely. (See my previous blogs, The Smell of Success and Fifty Shades of Outsourcing). Or, if you prefer, read the Rob Hughes article in The Guardian (9th of July). On that topic, I broke the news via Twitter, that the army were now controlling security lanes. I confirmed this in the Fifty Shades blog. I see tonight that further Argylls are now being trained, in civilian searches and the use of the x-ray scanners. I believe 250 have been allocated so far.

Buckles also appeared in the New Statesman, in April this year. You can see the full article here: (**38**).

He was asked a number of questions; these two (and the replies) caught my eye:
"5. Who is your business hero and why?
Margaret Thatcher, because in the early years she led the biggest economic turnaround in

recent history.

6. What should the government do to improve the UK business outlook?
To continue to focus on traditional Tory values around encouraging a meritocracy and inspiring value creation."

To me, this is simply trooping the colour, openly taking a political side. Considering the increasing involvement of G4S in policing and, the facts about the police reform agenda, that are becoming ever more apparent (See blog The History of The Future); this is causing me significant, further worry. In fact this goes deeper, adding weight to the concerns raised in, what I have dubbed, the 'Anti Winsor Report'; which can be viewed in full here: (**10**). It outlines a complex web of links between politicians, think tanks, security corporations and ACPO officers. It links all of this to the Winsor Report too.

This next site is the 'Corporate Watch' page with a brief 'who's who' section on G4S. (**39**). This site goes on, to give details of each individual's earnings and shares. Beneath that it says, and I quote:

"Buckles, Dighton and Gibson's remuneration is even more generous than those figures suggest as many of their G4S shares are paid into the company's Employee Benefit Trust.

Described by HMRC as 'tax avoidance, pure and simple'.

EBTs allow employees of a company to avoid a significant amount of tax. If the shares the company deposits in the trust on their behalf increase in value, that growth will be taxed as capital gains and therefore at 28%, rather than the income tax rate, which for high earners like Buckles and co. will be 45%. National insurance will also be avoided on the gains.

According to G4S' accounts, each of Nick Buckles, Trevor Dighton and Graham Gibson had a 'deemed interest in 6,265,571 ordinary shares held in the trust'. Employee Benefit Trusts have been described by HMRC as 'tax avoidance, pure and simple'. No wonder Buckles told the Daily Telegraph last year he never had any ambition of working for anyone else".

Of course, we all know an increasing amount about tax avoidance. Jimmy Carr, K2, Senior directors of the HMRC, Politicians. The list is growing.

At a slight tangent (but seriously worth looking into) take a look at that last link again...Lord Paul Condon is on there, former ACPO ranking officer, as covered in the Anti Winsor Report but who's that above him? Mark Seligman, Deputy Chairman, Non-Executive Director.

A former banker, Seligman juggles his G4S responsibilities with board membership of BG Group (the British Gas group of companies) and a directorship at Kingfisher PLC, as well as 'senior roles'...advising the government on decisions that G4S takes a 'particular interest' in.

He is the chairman of the Industrial Development Advisory Board (confirmed on their web site), a statutory body within the Department for Business, Innovation and Skills that "provides robust, independent, business advice to Ministers on large business investment decisions".

He is also a member of the Regional Growth Fund Advisory Panel (confirmed on their web site). This is a government appointed body, chaired by Michael Heseltine; the panel considers bids for funding for the government's £1.4 billion Regional Growth Fund. The fund's purpose is to "boost private sector growth in areas currently over dependent on the public sector".

Seligman is also an alternate member of the Panel on Takeovers and Mergers. The Panel describes its "central objective" as ensuring "fair treatment for all shareholders in takeover bids"; ironic given G4S' attempted takeover of ISS faltered, when shareholders bristled at the perceived unfairness of the bid.

Before all this, Seligman was a chartered accountant at PriceWaterhouseCoopers, and held senior roles at investment banks SG Warburg & Co, Barclays de Zoete, CSFB and Credit Suisse.

I hear that little alarm bell ringing once more. It said "senior roles advising Govt on decisions that G4S take particular interest in". It said "Chair of Industrial Development Board, providing robust, independent advice to Ministers". It also said "a member of the Regional Growth Fund, purpose to boost private sector growth in areas 'over' dependant on public sector". And this, on the CV of man clearly 'with' G4S; previously with Banks & PWC:
G4S Earnings: £82,000
G4S Shares: 75,000

Now, we come back to the G4S Regional Chief Exec for UK and Africa. Remember, he's the one who went on holiday with David Cameron to Africa last year, to drum up some business? As we know, his name is David Taylor-Smith, but he likes to be known as DTS.

His full name is, David James Benwell Taylor-Smith MBE, an honour he was awarded, alongside his wife Mrs Jacqueline Ann Hunter Taylor-Smith MBE in 2003, for charitable services overseas. He started life at Southampton University before taking up a short term commission in the Royal Dragoon Guards. He left with the rank of Captain.

On leaving the army, he had several offers of work, including acting as an assistant to then Tory politician Michael Hestletine, which he declined (There is nothing obvious, yet, that would suggest why he was offered that). He went on to do a variety of charity work overseas, including Operation Raleigh (due to his age he must have been a manager rather than a volunteer). I know very little about this but if you want to look it up, the site is here: (**40**) It is, however, quite relevant.

In 1994, DTS was appointed Hong Kong director of a sight saving charity called Project ORBIS. Whilst in Hong Kong, his next career stepping stone was to join Jardine Matheson a large Victorian conglomerate, in a conflict with the Chinese Govt, just as it was was due to take over sovereignty of Hong Kong.

DTS had the role of Corporate Communications Chief. Part of the conflict was over an area of dockland that had been allotted to Jardines and also, to their support of the Governor Chris Patten's election rules.

Chris Patten, the last Governor of Hong Kong (and former Conservative Party Chairman) took up his role there in 1992 until the hand over in June 1997. In the build up to the handover, there was intense political negotiations between China and the Conservative Foreign Secretary Malcolm Rifkind. Here's a handy summary: (**41**).

It seems inconceivable that 'DTS', in his role at Jardines, did not meet or have contact with Chris Patten or, quite probably, Malcolm Rifkind.

To quote my anonymous friend, who I have a lot of research to thank for, "this lad has been rubbing shoulders with Tory ministers since the 90's, or earlier".

Another quick detour, really quick this one. Did you know that Chris Patten is the current chairman of the BBC Trust? This is the BBC's governing body and sets the strategic direction. Also, did you know that Malcolm Rifkind is shown as patron of the Conservative Tory Reform Group? As well as being Chairman of the Intelligence and Security Committee.

He is also a patron of Raleigh International (which it became called after Op Raleigh).

That's what I like to call a secondary, or circular, link. I can't help but thinking that there is something very Jason Bourne about all of this.

Moving forwards, I've taken a closer look at the Capital Markets Day publications on the G4S website again, I've mentioned them before. (Smell of Success blog)

At this point, you may wish to sit down.

Bottom of page 3 to page 4:

"We've been asked a lot recently on what's our view on UK Government market dynamics in the wake of the General Election and the budget deficit? So I just want to give you our perspective on that. I think the backdrop of this is the first two points, irrespective of Labour, Conservative or Liberal our view is that the major parties, and I do include three major parties, have a belief in the role of the private sector. And that belief is that it does deliver change, it's definitely regarded as a useful tool to reform the public sector and value for money. So with that as the backdrop our view is that timing will be important in terms of the General Election. We have a sizeable budget deficit to address, we believe that you may see a diminishing of capital programmes, PFI, and you will see a drive to reconfigure public services in bold ways. And I think that will see us talking about anything from business process outsourcing activity, through to asset sales, or investment in Gov Co's."

Page 4:

"So in the last three or four months we've been engaged in conversations with different areas of Government that would have been unthinkable a year ago, at having anything from an interest in acquiring joint venturing or looking at ways that we can significantly reduce areas of Government spend."

I'm getting seriously freaked out now, at the crystal balls people seem to be able to purchase these days. Nick Herbert, with Blair Gibbs, wrote many of the Winsor recommendations in 2007 (see recent blog The History of the Future). G4S were saying all this back in 2010. It's rather spooky.

Page 6:

"In police we're having some very interesting conversations with the police. We've always been slightly short term pessimistic on police and long term optimistic.

The short term pessimistic is buying behaviour is not well configured for large decision, because of the 43 forces. But actually if you stood back and said what's the macro trend? Well it is towards more outsourcing. And we now have a significant police business, delivering a range of services in what they want.

And that tends to be anything from quite tactical services in individual services to now forces acting in coalition with two or three forces.

Our encouragement to the Government is, look
scale this up at a national level, pick some big
areas and then outsource a programme of
activity."

Encouragement to the Government, back in
2010? Clearly they listened.

But how do you encourage a Government?
Well, I suppose think tanks are just one way of
creating influential policy. That's what they say
themselves remember. Coalitions of forces
sounds very familiar too. East of England
forces, Surrey and West Midlands. (If you refer
back to 'The Question of Nepotism' you'll see
another circular link, between this and the
Winsor Report).

In fact, thanks to FOI, Hertfordshire Police
Authority were recently asked this:
   "I have read in the press that you, together
with Bedfordshire and Cambridgeshire, are
seeking to use a private company, G4S, to
provide your HR, Finance and Information &
Communications Technology (ICT) services.
Can you please tell me a) The scope of services
you envisage being transferred to G4S b)
Whether or not this proposal has been put out to

tender and the identities of all bidders c) The annual cost you anticipate will be saved from your budget by transferring these services to G4S"

They were clearly prepared for this line of questioning, as the response was provided in an uncharacteristic twenty-four hours.

"1. The scope of the services covers Organisational Support which comprises the following functions:
HR (including Learning and Development), Finance and Payroll, ICT, Procurement, Corporate Communications, Corporate Services/Corporate Development, Estates and Facilities, Fleet, Legal Services, Business Support.
2. The proposal is to use an existing framework contract managed by Lincolnshire Police Authority. This framework contract was put out to full competitive European tender by Lincolnshire Police Authority. Hertfordshire Police Authority was named on the original Official Journal of the European Union (OJEU) notice. Hertfordshire Police Authority had no involvement in the selection process of G4S and thus any further enquires on this aspect would need to be directed to Lincolnshire Police Authority.

3. At this time, it is not possible to say what savings we expect to make through using this contract. This is because detailed contract discussions are now taking place and it would prejudice these discussions to reveal a figure".

The answers to 1 and 3 are fairly explanatory but number 2...what does that mean exactly? The implication is not pretty. Another anonymous friend puts it like this, a way that's very simple to understand:

"Whilst Lincolnshire may well have fulfilled their EU tender obligations and selected G4S, how does that entitle other Police Authorities to piggy-back on that contract? Surely each Police Authority or each partnership, as in this case, should tender their business separately? If they can all hang off the back of the first Authority (i.e. Lincolnshire) with no further tendering, G4S have got it all tied up and privatisation is well and truly here".

Others, who have seen this FOI, match my own concern; It seems that Hertfordshire are determined to use G4S, without having specified any part of the framework contract themselves and, with no apparent clue as to whether they will even save any money.

Page 55:

"Q David Hancock, Morgan Stanley: Just one follow up on Julian's questions on government for David. You mentioned I think discussions around buying or investing in government assets, and talking about things that a year ago weren't conceivable now are starting to be talked about. Can you just give us some examples of that please?

David Taylor-Smith: On the first one I wish I could describe those conversations but I don't think I should.
Nick Buckles: I don't think you should either.
David Taylor-Smith: Because they are conversations which are happening prior to, during and immediately after the election, during the purdah period. And they are senior civil servants who've been asked to get on and draw up contingency plans around budget deficit activity. And I don't think it's appropriate to kind of mention those. But they are interesting conversations that a year ago you just wouldn't be having."

If you are not in the know: Purdah is the common term used to describe the pre-election period, used in United Kingdom politics to describe the time between an announced election and the final election result. The time period offers a prior opportunity for government departments to develop guidance and policy due to any impact resulting from the election. It also prevents central and local government departments from making announcements about any new or controversial government initiatives (such as modernisation initiatives, administrative and legislative changes) which could be seen to be advantageous to any candidates or parties in the forthcoming election, or which may commit any incoming new administration to policies which it wouldn't support.

Exactly how close to these senior civil servants and their 'unspeakable' plans were G4S? I know for a fact there are some worried people at the Home Office and they are not liking questions. (Please see previous blog The Sound of Panic for a quite clear example).

Service, Ministry of Justice, UK Boarders Agency. And what's very pleasing for those of you that were here a year or so ago with the Department of Work and Pensions we said that is going to be a target area for us and we've grown the Department of Work and Pensions, this doesn't include our Welfare to Work wins, when that's clocked in next year that will be £130 million."

A quick note, I've seen the Policy Exchange report on W2W (*Welfare to Work*) being criticised today due to its lack of evidential basis. Apparently the author only visited two job centres. Again I believe this points to a further, potential, link between the think tanks, corporations and government policy. (also see the Anti Winsor Report).

Page 39:
Without direct quote, you see a, just signed, major extension to security provision that's one of the largest commercial customers, Royal Bank of Scotland (RBS). As you can see here: (**42**) 84% of RBS is owned by the Government, by taxpayers. So effectively we already pay G4S for this.

Page 41:
   "So we will be responsible for three areas for

managing subcontractors as a prime to get long term unemployed people who have been out of work for more than one year back into work and being paid on the basis of that. We see this as providing significant additional growth opportunities.

Two nights ago I was with Iain Duncan Smith, Oliver Letwin, Crispin Blunt and they're talking now also applying this into the prisons programmes, into drug programmes and also benefit fraud."

I must say at this juncture, this is all looks very cosy. It must be nice. It does however make me wonder, about those event workers under the bridge...it also makes me start to wonder about some of the third sector, or charity, ventures that have been upping the ante of late.

Page 42:
   "You see on the right an interesting acquisition, we just made a couple of months ago Cotswold Group, the largest surveillance company in Europe particularly traditional in insurance markets. But we see that as having - they've got some very clever analytics that we could then use that leverage into the government space around fraud detection (or police intelligence and evidence gathering that

has been tendered out)."

Well. What can I say to add anything to that? It's very clear. They are ready for a lot more than just vehicle fleet management and custody suites.

Page 43:
"We see increasing evidence that the government are looking for outsourcing. This has changed in the last three months; we're having some very interesting conversations now with government on future programmes. And those are either doing more of what we currently do; prisons or new stuff in new areas using models like neutrals. So we're looking, I had a conversation with the government last week about an area of government they're interested in us forming or private sector forming a joint venture with as a method of outsourcing. So it's really interesting innovative stuff coming down the tubes".

They say interesting stuff coming down the tubes; I see the truth coming out of the spout. The links with the government are far too close and this makes me understand the recent targeted spin, about the police being a monopoly service. Make it look like it is a monopoly already, to disguise (in plain sight) the real monopoly being built. This is simple reverse psychology.

Page 59:

"Q (re B'ham prison) Andrew Ripper, Merrill Lynch: So just in terms of giving us a sense of order of magnitude what sort of costs you'd expect to run at or manning levels versus what the original position was?

David Taylor-Smith: Probably a bit sensitive, we're just starting yesterday and running on for the next two weeks what's technically called announcing our measures to the staff in Birmingham and it might be a little bit sensitive if I was to give you that before we told the staff so.

Nick Buckles: Was the press release from the government not highlighting the savings over a period of time? It was, wasn't it?

David Taylor-Smith: Yeah so Ken Clarke highlighted it but I mean we're talking about a significant reduction in staffing."

And there is the Modus Operandi; increase profitability by reducing costs. Apply this to policing, where 80% is workforce, and what do you get? Listen carefully...yes, cuts. That nasty little truth, that is being spun like a kid on waltzer. They should take some advice: if you spin too much, it will make you ill.

organisations and also with government bodies".

This is particularly interesting *tell*, they know the key is not political pressure, as PCCs are clearly showing; the public don't really want politics linked to policing. So it's nice all round to have a back up plan. If PCCs are the front door way to drive partnering arrangements into police forces, backed up by the Value For Money HMIC...then budget reductions are waiting at the back door, backed up by private companies, ready to kick it in and get busy while people are looking out the front.

Again as a quick side note, I had a particularly interesting encounter last week with a PCC candidate, who comes from a charity, NACRO. They manage offenders, homelessness, that kind of thing. One of his key aims is to further the involvement of the third sector. The force he is running to be head of is in a ten year contract with G4S already. Lincolnshire. G4S described the Lincolnshire contract as 'market changing'.

Interestingly, we know they were represented by White and Case in this contract and, in May 2011, the Home Office said that the firm would be paid for Tom Winsor's time; as he independently reviewed policing. As it turns out they never got the £104,000 and, have issued a statement saying there never was such an agreement.

Back to PCCs and the third sector; read in this new context, my three 'The Definition of a PCC' blogs take on a whole new aspect. Anyone would think that I picked my explorations very carefully indeed. In short, what I'm seeing here is a great, tremendous team effort. Well done; tea and medals all round.

Page 42:
   "Q Andrew Ripper, Merrill Lynch: I've got a couple if I may. First of all just in terms of the police bidding activity, can you talk about what sort of returns profile you think you can get on the Lincs contract?
Nick Buckles, Group CEO: Yeah I think on the returns side we're looking for the high single digits after 12 months that would be our expectation, we won't get there straight away but that's the sort of level".

So that's 8% or 9% after year one is out of the way? This tells me that:
a) This really is all about profit
and;

b) The immediate loss of 60 staff confirms they meant what they said earlier.

All of the transcripts to these Capital Market Days can be found on the G4S website here: (**44**).

When I previously wrote, that this was a very deep rabbit hole, I was not joking. I hope you can now see why. It would be very easy for me, down here in the darkness, to blow this little candle out and stop looking; fade into the shadows myself. The bottom line is I can't. I Won't.

Because I have sworn an oath, to do what needs to be done. It does not rest. It does not sleep. It gives little back. Because I have been reminded, of the ultimate gravity of that responsibility. Because, even on the days when a storm blows around me, I have to carry on; even with a heavy heart and a saddened soul. Because I must keep my emotions in check, stay keen in my focus; even when the words of others, are a tinderbox in the hay barn.

I'm casting the light, as far and wide as I can. We must all continue to do so. Because, in this darkening world, the good deeds must shine brighter than ever.

The Battle Cry:

"There are many who need be to be held to account.
There is much truth still buried"

14th of July 2012

Well, this has been a hell of a week. I've watched the penny, the one I've been chasing, start to drop. In quite a spectacular way. If anyone forgets G4S in a hurry, I'll be surprised but I maintain; this is just the tip of a very deep and blackened iceberg. For that reason I have no choice but to carry on falling down this rabbit hole.

Today I stumbled across a song which, for me, has become an anthem, for PFTP (**44**). We hear people, in positions where we expect more, telling us that everything is alright, all the time. Easy for them to say. But, one of these days, it wont be so easy for them to maintain.

We have evolved far beyond expectation. Police For The Public. Public For The Police. PFTP. Out of nowhere, out of nothing, a force to be truly reckoned with and, one that is reaching out to and engaging with the public at all levels. I never thought I'd see so many different people united, against a common danger and working toward a common goal; doing the right thing by the public.

What we have achieved is startling and, frankly, amazing. It owes a lot and, is a testament to, a growing group of passionate individuals who believe that honesty and integrity comes above all else. All of us are risking something yet we all stand together. That alone restores my faith in many things.

Today however is about relaxing, regrouping, taking in the impact of the week; moving forwards in a way that makes sure people don't mistake a small victory, for the end of a war.

We are fighting for the future of not only the police service, but for a service for everyone.

Without the police, the last independent office that enables individuals to challenge things like the G4S débâcle, the final barrier will be gone and: the rule of politics and deceit will be unchallengeable. Personally, I am in full flow. I have research ongoing, which is pretty bulky and I'm also bringing together everything that has gone before, into one place, so that everyone can get their noodle around it.

Despite that, I still have time; to make cakes, to read my children bed time stories. To ignore the rules of the semi colon at will. I want to leave you to enjoy your weekend, to enjoy what we have achieved, what can be done through sheer determination.

Before I do though, I want to share this, a Churchillian battle cry, from a very decent PFTP member:

"Even though large tracts of Policing have fallen to PCC's/G4$ and the grip of the Tories and their odious apparatus, the "Policy Exchange". We shall not flag or fail. We shall go on to the end.

We shall fight them in Whitehall...... and on the streets of London. With growing confidence, we shall defend the independent office of "Constable", whatever the cost. We will fight them in their G4$ boardrooms. We will fight them in their tax havens.

We will fight them on their blogs and twitter feeds. We will fight their anti-police media spin. And we will NEVER surrender.

And should their forces subjugate and discipline us, then our friends, families and allies will carry on the struggle. And, in God's good time, the new world, with all its power and might will rescue and liberate them."

Make no mistake, this is not done. There are many who need be to be held to account. There is much truth still buried. We must be brave and, be bold. Evil things can only happen when the good stand and do nothing. We stand and we DO. What other choice is there Rest well, get ready and, together, let's make doing the right thing count.

The Acceptance of Fate:

"Before the G4S story is buried in spin and manoeuvres, resignations and reshuffles: we must pursue all of the loose ends"

16th of July 2012

Marcus Aelius Aurelius Verus Caesar was born on the 26th of April 121A.D. His stoic tome Meditations, was written in Greek, while on campaign, between 170 and 180. It is still revered as a literary monument, to a philosophy of service and duty; describing how to find and preserve equanimity, in the midst of conflict, by following nature as a source of guidance and inspiration.

He is regarded as the last of "the five good emperors", a phrase coined by the political philosopher Niccolò Machiavelli in 1503.
   "From the study of this history we may also learn how a good government is to be established; for while all the emperors who succeeded to the throne by birth, except Titus, were bad, all were good who succeeded by adoption, as in the case of the five from Nerva to Marcus.
But as soon as the empire fell once more to the heirs by birth, its ruin recommenced".

Machiavelli argued that these adopted emperors, through good rule, earned the respect of those around them:
   "Titus, Nerva, Trajan, Hadrian, Antoninus, and Marcus had no need of praetorian cohorts, or of countless legions to guard them, but were

defended by their own good lives, the good-will of their subjects".

Marcus Aurelius died on the 17th of March 180 A.D. without seeing his birthplace, Rome, again. He speaks volumes to me, in what he wrote, what history says he stood for; even in the date of his death. Aside from the quite pertinent relevance of Machiavelli, at present, something else attributed to him leaps out at me. It is this:

"Accept the things to which fate binds you, and love the people with whom fate brings you together, but do so with all your heart."

If you know anything about me by now, then you will have an idea what this means to me; who else it refers to. It encapsulates PFTP and, is further underlined by Marcus Aurelius' own philosophy. Service and duty. I was not born in Rome, but near the south coast of England; I grew there and have always understood a fundamental rule of nature: that the tide always turns.

The week just gone, the tide was for us; now it will be against us once more. Before it pulls out too far, we must chase it; then next time we must let it do some of the work, ride it, all the way back to the shore. From turn of tide, to the first breakers on the sand. Before the G4S story is buried in spin and manoeuvres, resignations and reshuffles: we must pursue all of the loose ends.

We see these things happening clearly already. Nick Buckles seems likely to resign, with a goodbye kiss of around £21 million; clearly G4S will then be fixed and we can all return to blind trust again. Jeremy Hunt has become useful again, having just escaped from Leveson questions on lobbying, by the skin of his teeth; making appearances now, saying that G4S were honest and came clean. I believe the word humble may have been used.

Hunt is a good choice as a potential sacrificial lamb, his departure would appease many and, in that slight of hand, everything will be okay again. The danger is, that G4S are not the only privatisation provider and Hunt not the only MP tainted by lobbyists. In the Commons, to the laughter of her peers, the Home Secretary says its all okay and she didn't know it was an issue. In private the Defence Secretary is rumoured to call the 'P45 Privates' the "Ring of Fired".

Make no mistake, this is not isolated and will not go away. This basket of snakes will

perpetuate their survival in anyway they can.
There are other providers, just waiting in the
wings. They and the politicians, will use all the
wiles at their disposal: ignorance, wolves
dressed as sheep, deridement, ricidule, snide
attack and open assault. They will do this
because the lid on the basket has been opened
and; they are not happy with the exposure.

When snakes are scared, they bite. With all
their venom. Against this backdrop, we can
wait for tidal changes no more. Too much is at
stake. So, taking some guidance from nature
amidst this conflict and, accepting fate, the
thing to which I am now bound: I chase the
tide.

Lobbying is an issue and the players are known,
the charities, the think tanks, the corporations
who sponsor them and also, the PR firms who
specialise in getting access. Only days ago,
MPs were still raising their concerns, after
government plans had been made to water
down new regulations against it.

"All lobbyists, including charities, think tanks
and unions, should be subject to new lobbying
regulation, a group of MPs have said. They
criticised government plans to bring in a
statutory register for third-party lobbyists, such
as PR firms, only. They said the plan would "do

274

nothing to improve transparency". (**46**).

Apparently, it's actually as simple as getting a parliamentary pass and having some change in your pocket (**47**):

"In the House of Commons cafeteria you can theoretically gain the ear of an MP for the price of a cup of tea. The issue, then, is how to get in. One option is to obtain a parliamentary pass, which allows flexible entry to common areas of Parliament with no need to register any meetings you might have with politicians"

In fact, it is even said:

"... there was a clear spike in the number of lobby groups with financial clients entertaining ministers' special advisers as the 2011 Finance Bill was passing through the House of Commons".

I just cannot reconcile this type of activity with charity, as I understand it:

charity
noun
plural **charities**
1.Provision of help or relief to the poor; alms giving.
2.Something given to help the needy; alms.
3.An institution, organization, or fund established to help the needy.

I can't see how this help for the needy - what I think of in terms of Saturday, with my nan in the Oxfam on the High Street - can possibly have anything to do with this:

"A think tank (or policy institute) is an organization that conducts research and engages in advocacy in areas such as social policy, political strategy, economics, military, technology issues and in the creative and cultural field. Most think tanks are non-profit organizations, which some countries such as the United States and Canada provide with tax exempt status. Other think tanks are funded by governments, advocacy groups, or businesses, or derive revenue from consulting or research work related to their projects"

This is neither buying a second hand tartan skirt, nor digging a well in Africa is it?

Oscar Wilde said that charity creates a multitude of sins; read on and you may agree with my opinion: That a multitude of sins create charities.

And its not exactly that these think tanks can be considered completely transparent in how they are funded: (**47**). If the Policy Exchange was a boiler...I'd be scrapping it.

Britain."

Reform was launched by Andrew Haldenby and Nick Herbert and Patrick Barbour in 2002. In October 2001 The Times reported having seen a strategy document for the future think-tank which stated that it would be modelled closely on Washington's Heritage Foundation. The article reported that Reform would be launched in the New Year, i.e. early 2002.

Reform was incorporated as a not for profit company on 4 December 2001 under the name Reform Britain. The Daily Telegraph reported that it was run by its founders Andrew Haldenby and Nick Herbert, as well as media executive James Bethell.
In May 2004 reform registered an associated charity the Reform Research Trust. Amongst the new charity's objectives were to:
   "educate the public on public policy issues, in particular in relation to public services and the economy".

Of course Nick Herbert is the Crime and Justice Minister, leading the current reform agenda in policing, you know, political layering of PCCs, privatisation of police forces and yes, he did write the Winsor Report, in 2007 Blair Gibbs. It's quite aptly explained in my previous blog

"The History of the Future". Gibbs went on to become his chief of staff before moving to the Policy Exchange, where Nick Herbert now regularly takes part in sponsored events. One such 'do', recently, was a Deloitte sponsored event on PCCs, which I describe in "

Citi Group	£15,000.00
PA Consulting	£15,000.00
PWC	£15,000.00
Telereal Trillium	£15,000.00
Benenden Healthcare Society	£14,250.00
Capita Symonds	£13,500.00
R3	£13,500.00
Airwave	£12,500.00
G4S	£12,500.00
Novo Nordisk	£12,500.00
RSA	£12,500.00
Home Group	£12,000.00
NHS Confederation	£12,000.00
Vodafone	£12,000.00
Cicero	£10,000.00
ICAEW	£10,000.00
MITIE	£10,000.00
TheCityUK	£10,000.00
BG Group	£7,500.00
Birmingham City Council	£7,500.00
Cable & Wireless	£7,500.00
Centrica plc	£7,500.00
CII	£7,500.00
City of London	£7,500.00
E&Y	£7,500.00
GSK	£7,500.00
Maximus	£7,500.00
McKinsey	£7,500.00
Merck	£7,500.00

Optical Confederation	£7,500.00
Sodexo	£7,500.00
Unum	£7,500.00
Circle Housing Group	£6,500.00
Finnamore	£6,500.00
BVCA	£6,000.00
Cerner	£6,000.00
Collinson Grant	£6,000.00
BP	£5,000.00
Circle	£5,000.00
Milliman	£5,000.00
UnitedHealth UK	£5,000.00

Another think tank is Localis.

Localis, officially Localis Research Ltd, is a right-wing think-tank focused on local government. Along with Policy Exchange – with which it is closely associated – it has been central to the development of Tory thinking on local government and a legitimising political rhetoric stressing local accountability juxtaposed with bureaucratic and dictatorial central government. Localis was set up in late 2001 by three senior Conservatives counsellors; Lord Hanningfield, Colin Barrow and Paul Bettison. It was incorporated as a company limited by guarantee (i.e. without shareholders) on 14 September 2001 and was launched on or around 3 October 2001.

All three founders were powerful figures in local government. Lord Hanningfield, who was later charged under the Theft Act for his Parliamentary Expenses claims, was the Leader of Essex County Council and vice-chairman of the Local Government Association. He was appointed Chairman. Colin Barrow, a millionaire businessman, was then a senior member of Suffolk County Council and chairman of the Local Government Improvement and Development Agency (IDEA). Paul Bettison was a member of the executive of the Local Government Association and leader of Bracknell Forest Borough Council.

In 2003 it relocated to 10 Storeys Gate where Policy Exchange and Conservatives for Change were based. Policy Exchange and Localis then began to collaborate on research. Policy Exchange's accounts, filed with the Charity Commission, report payments from Localis to cover joint research projects starting in 2003. The following amounts were received by Policy Exchange between 2003 and 2007: 2003 - £10,297; 2004 - £15,035; 2005 - £30,000; 2006 - £14,250 and 2007 - £20,000.

From February 2003 the serving directors of Policy Exchange have also served on the board of Localis; first Nicholas Boles, then his successor Anthony Browne, and finally Neil O'Brien. Explain the cluster of them at Clutha House. Spitting distance of parliament and their founders. I can't think of a really effective way of describing this, so I have looked in a dictionary and found this, which seems appropriate:

2012:

"As a major police authority, PA's client provides over-arching governance and jurisdiction for over 1500 police officers and a population of 600,000. In response to a 20% cut in government funding the police authority needed to implement a change programme that would transform volume crime operations* to improve the service provided to its citizens at an overall reduced cost." (**48**).

I have to say, seeing the Reform link now does make me wonder, just a little bit more...but then, if you clicked through to the Slip of the Mask link earlier, I think I made my concerns about consultants quite clear.

Back from the brief detour, it does really seem that these think tanks are a bit of a murky mess, all very friendly to say the least. It's also weird how the questions go unanswered. I'm still waiting for a reply to the email that I sent to Nick Herbert on the 20th of June...in it all I asked was this:
1) It seems, from the event this week, that it was sponsored by consultancy Deloitte. Tell me what their interest was? I am aware that you have a good relationship with the Exchange and your former Staff Officer Blair Gibbs, so he may be able to provide you with additional

information should you need it to reply effectively. And, tell me how much did Deloitte contribute to the event? Please also explain your relationship with the Policy Exchange and how this has influenced you in mapping out police reform; if at all.

2) What is your knowledge of 'ADS' and their function in representing the interests of numerous corporations in security? What was their interest in sponsoring the recent policing futures event? How much did they contribute, financially, to the event?

3) Including your time at Reform, how much contact have you had with G4S? Please try and be specific.

Were G4S or other companies such as Serco making any kind of financial contribution to Reform?

If so, how much, from when exactly and, how regularly. If you could again clarify why they contribute, that would be of great help in explaining this.

4) Please outline in detail your personal experience as regards to policing.

Of course, G4S is now a hot potato, but thanks to Who Funds You, I have at least part of the answer. It seems it's either silence or spin. No other option.

relies on the fact that private companies can pledge to deliver,' Mr Gibbs said. 'Companies should only contract what they can deliver and citing exceptional circumstances is no excuse."

I refuse to pay to read it, especially when I can read this (**49**) for free, from before the issue became a radioactive spud:

"Far from eroding the public policing function, private companies could bolster it. Private involvement in policing is already widespread, and greater use of civilians has improved services and reduced waste. In many areas, civilians have freed up resources otherwise spent on expensive officers to do jobs in business support and control rooms that do not require warranted powers.
Our research supports the view of Ian Blair
(

be seen as an opportunity, not a threat".

Of course, one of the keys to good financial management is to have a good accountant. Like this one (**50**) HW Fisher describes itself as:

"a commercially astute organisation with a personal, partner-led service aimed at entrepreneurial small, medium enterprises (SMEs), large corporates and high-net worth individuals. Our clients come from many different backgrounds and are active in all branches of commerce and industry. Our reputation is grounded in quality, delivering premium advisory services efficiently and cost-effectively. Our fee income ranks us as a mid-tier top 25 UK chartered accountancy firm."

I'd never heard of them and wouldn't have but for one tiny thing, a postcode. NW1 3ER. It's weird, when I was looking at the think tanks, Localis and Policy Exchange, they are all listed in Westminster, spitting distance from the Houses of Parliament.
Which is high rent although good for a cup of tea but, they have registered addresses in NW1 3ER, which is in Camden.

This made me doubly curious, although registered addresses are not uncommon. So I bought the 2011 accounts, for all three think tanks, for download. You don't need to though, the summary on Policy Exchange alone is interesting enough, look it up on any free company check website. I learned two things.

Firstly, that Localis owes the Policy Exchange £21 and Secondly, what restricted funds are:

"Grants or donations that require that the funds be used in a specific way or for a specific purpose. They can be considered a contract between the donating party and the receiving party. Restricted funds are often associated with non-profit organisations, since a donation might be made to the organisation for a specific use only".

One practical example would be: I donate £15.00 to Oxfam to buy a part of a 'well drill' and only that. Oxfam accept the donation and can only buy that specified part. Another practical example would be this: I donate £15,000 to Policy Exchange, specifically requesting that they write a paper, that will suggest that it's a good idea for the public sector to outsource a function, in my specific business area. Because it's a restricted fund that's all they could do with it.

In 2011 Policy Exchange took income in donations of around £1.8 million and, of that,

£1.1 million was in restricted, which they don't declare the purpose of in their accounts either. I believe it is here that the tea drinking is key.

Please note, I'm not even going to explain tax avoidance or tax evasion, or the tax benefits of donations to charities; or indeed the fact that changes to charity donation limits were fought hard against. I know that we've all heard enough about that of late that it requires no recap from me.

So, for now, I'm going to leave you with these thoughts and, once you have digested them, read this once more: The Little Light in The Darkness. Then, if you must, go back to the start of this blog and read up on lobbying once more.

Has the context slapped you in the face with a wet fish? Can anyone, hand on heart, tell me that any of this sounds right? Normal? Wholesome?

...that is one deafeningly silent reply.

Even David Cameron said this was the next big scandal waiting to happen. I can't disagree with his assessment. It's quite clear that MPs are aware of this and, that even the Prime Minister is aware, that this issue exists. If they weren't concerned this could cause serious problems, it would never have even come into review. It is however only

The Clubs That Exist:

See here (**54**) for an item from their website.

with 'three of my favourite politicians',

publication of the register.

revealed that members of the government had attended invitation-only events organised by the Chemistry Club. The Guardian reported: Companies have been paying up to £1,800 a head to meet ministers, senior government advisers and MPs at a series of networking events previously banned by the Cabinet Office.

The chief secretary to the Treasury, Danny Alexander, policing minister, Nick Herbert, and climate change minister, Lord Taylor, have all addressed the exclusive invite-only events, organised by a networking business called the Chemistry Club, and usually hosted at the high-end Sartoria restaurant in Mayfair, London. Senior MPs from backbench committees have also attended the events, as have senior civil servants and special advisers from the Treasury, Home Office, Ministry of Defence, Department of Energy and Climate Change and other key departments.

At an event in October 2011, Danny Alexander, along with civil servants from the Department of Health, the Ministry of Defence and Department of Energy and Climate Change, met with representatives of energy companies EDF and Gazprom, defence manufacturer EADS and communications giants Vodafone and Google. Tamasin Cave of SpinWatch said "Lobbying is a tactical investment which affects companies' bottom line – they do not spend £1,800 for nothing".

The Cabinet Office had previously issued guidance to departments back in August 2010 informing civil servants not to attend Chemistry Club events. However, The Guardian revealed that public figures from governmental departments and public bodies, including the Metropolitan Police and GCHQ, had attended Chemistry Club events as soon as one month after the guidance had been given.

Following discussions with the Chemistry Club the Cabinet Office subsequently overturned its previous ruling and civil servants were once more allowed to attend events organised by the networking company. Labour's Shadow Cabinet Office Minister, Jon Trickett MP, said "These revelations leave serious questions for David Cameron to answer if he is to avoid the suspicion that lobbyists believe they can buy influence with his government."

Past speakers at the Chemistry Club's IT Forum include:
Chief Constable Sir Hugh Orde, President, ACPO

Professor Nigel Shadbolt, Information Advisor, HM Government
Sir Ian Andrews, Chairman, SOCA (Serious Organised Crime Agency)
Dr Vince Cable MP, Secretary of State for Business, Innovation and Skills
The Rt. Hon Francis Maude MP, Minister for the Cabinet Office and Paymaster General."

evenings, and are invited to signal who they

million of public money to a charity for which

The Truth of The Matter:

"reasonable grounds to believe that this year's pork
pie awards may not be heading in the direction of
Melton Mowbray"

please understand that I just cannot reply even if I want to...and I do.

I am bound by my promise to the regulations and, the regulations are law. I promised I would uphold it. There is nothing more or less to this. This is one of the most misunderstood things about what I do and, what it creates, is clear for all to see. Thank you for your patience and understanding.

Having just read the LOCOG response to the G4S/Olympics debacle, I have reasonable grounds to believe that this year's pork pie awards may not be heading in the direction of Melton Mowbray. Paul Deighton of LOCOG had these two things to say, in his written reply to the HASC:

"Since the signing of the contract in 2010, a series of weekly and other regularly scheduled meetings attended by Government, G4S and LOCOG have been held to monitor G4S' performance under the contract. In early April 2012, an additional weekly meeting led by senior management involving the Home Office, G4S and LOCOG was instigated in response to concerns which had been identified with the format and content of management information provided by G4S."

"Nick Buckles, David Taylor-Smith [CEO of G4S in the UK and Africa] and Ian Horseman-Sewell [G4S' global events specialist] confirmed to LOCOG on the morning of 11 July 2012 that, despite ongoing and recent assurances orally and in writing to the contrary, G4S would not be able to meet its labour pool target. LOCOG immediately contacted Home Office colleagues whereupon the issue was formally discussed at a meeting of the Olympic Security Board" [which took place at 11.30 am on that same day]."

And;
"Following G4S' statement at the Olympic Security Board on 11 July 2012 that it could not meet its labour pool targets, it was agreed among all the parties present that the Home Office would immediately proceed to request the MoD supply Armed Forces personnel to meet the shortfall acknowledged by G4S."
I chuckled reading this and, also finally understood that LOCOG must be a 'down with the kids' version of Low Cognition. LowCog for short.

Let's get this straight: Throughout the contract, weekly and scheduled meetings have taken place. Since April, weekly senior level meetings were in place because they weren't happy with information. And, suddenly, on the 11th of July, a day after my last G4S blog in the morning and media coverage from lunch time, G4S said

Now, I have other potential Melton Mowbrays to look into.

You may remember, back in 2011, a FOI response that stated White and Case would be reimbursed for Tom Winsor's time. Here it is: (**58**)

Of course, once it became clear that White and Case had represented G4S in the £200 million Lincolnshire contract, as the review was done, it became an issue. The Home Secretary had this to say:
  "Tom Winsor did his review entirely independently. He did not do that review as part of the firm - he did it as an individual". That's from this BBC News article here: (**59**)

So we move on, to the pre-appointment hearing of the HMIC where in response to the question from Keith Vaz, Mr Winsor revealed he has never received money. White and Case then disagreed with the Home Office's 2011 statement, saying they were never going to be paid anything, because it was Tom Winsor as an individual. You can read the rather abrupt letter here: (**60**)

The feeling I get, is that no one wants to be touched by this particular barge pole. Well all of this got me thinking...why would you do 349 days work for free? Well, not free actually, he did claim over £3000 in expenses: (**61**).

A cynical person would think that this whole, we'll pay the firm, no, the person, fox trot only came about because a whopping conflict of interest came out in public. Of course, my other concerns are well documented in this blog but; this whole, gap year, work for free, appointment with a huge salary at the end, privatisation goals in mind, scenario bothers me.

It's a real niggle that I have had and I am not alone.

In fact, it seems, there are very few, normal, members of the public who would do anything like this. I can tell you this, without doubt, because some have been asked. Yesterday, this question was put out to the public by a curious civilian:

mortgage to pay & couldn't work a month never mind a year w/o pay.

Builder 2 - less chatty. He said, "no. Ok, Bye"

Plumber 1 - was a no, couldn't afford to.

Plumber 2 - appeared to talk himself into believing the offer was real. He really wanted to be able to say yes, but couldn't work the year w/o pay first.

Accountant 1 - 'why would you work for no pay? No'

Accountant 2 - No! They have office staff to think about paying!"

So that's a unanimous and resounding "NO", from three separate trades. It seems that no reasonable, average person, would (or could) work a year for free, even to become the national head of their own trade at the end of it. Can you imagine the answer being different, if the offer had been to head up a trade, that they knew little about? I simply cannot.

I wonder...has Theresa May been reading the draft versions of my blogs?

The reason I ask is this breaking news: (**62**)

Yes, it seems the Pork Pie Award does go to LOCOG and the Home Office. My apologies to Melton Mowbray.

Normally, I am quite willing to forgive but with the weight of lies being told and the truth only coming out, because it was escaping anyway...I can neither forgive nor forget. Nor indeed can I claim to have even an ounce of trust left. Sadly, I believe the timing of this breaking news was no coincidence either. Just think about it. Really think, about what it came after and, don't allow your strings to be pulled.

Where there is smoke, there's fire.

The Politics of The Impossible:

"a weapon; used by those who are meddling in the
police service"

26th of July 2012

I have read something a few times now, since first seeing it mentioned.

It is this:
   "Police Regulations 2003 - Schedule 1:
1. A member of a police force shall at all times abstain from any activity which is likely to interfere with the impartial discharge of his duties or which is likely to give rise to the impression amongst members of the public that it may so interfere; and in particular a member of a police force shall not take any active part in politics."

I understand it was put out as a warning to officers, to make sure they didn't get tripped up. I'm sure it was done with the best of intentions but, shortly after it appeared, it became a weapon; used by those who are meddling in the police service. I am talking about the stone cold unaccountable. They know who they are. In fact I would say, it's quite funny they should sell the 'don't take sides in politics' message.

As my nan used to say, people in glass houses.

What I have been mulling over is, now that PCCs are a legal entity in policing, how can these 9 year old regulations possibly be compatible? They say the law is an ass, I say this particular regulation is a real donkey. It has been referenced, cited even, as a way of ensuring that the voices of desperate officers, outraged by what is being done and trapped with no rights, are finally silenced. If this legislation remains unchanged then all we have is a force of the state; the policing by consent model ended. Without any consultation.

I've broken down the elements of this and proffer my own thoughts:
   "A member of a police force shall at all times abstain from any activity which is likely to interfere with the impartial discharge of his duties"

In response to this I have chosen to abstain from having anything to do with official requests made by PCCs, because by their very existence and role, they will force me to breach this. This may sound ridiculous but this regulation binds me to that decision. Think it through. I must however speak to them otherwise I could be deemed as rude or as purposefully excluding a definable group. Both of these are big no-nos. And anything but impartial. What a predicament this is...

I also pondered another question on this very broad schedule. Say for example you were on a scheme which required you to bit and bob from department to department to achieve career goals quickly, or to tick boxes, or if your job was to keep crime figures down? Surely then you can't be impartial either; because you have to serve that need, first and foremost. Making you partisan by virtue of the very activity you are engaged in. Now there's a catch 22 for you.

If you take it as broadly as it's written you can't support Chelsea because you would breach this by rooting for them while on football duties. You can't go to a shoplifting at Tesco without going to Asda, Sainsbury and others before going back to Tesco again.
You can't only police one ward, you can't be a member of any staff associations, no pin badges, no focus groups...because it is any activity. ANY.

"or which is likely to give rise to the impression amongst members of the public that it may so interfere"

I have posted this, my refusal to have anything to do with PCCs, to my blog; so that there is a public record of the fact that I don't want their politics to meddle with my impartial role. That should prevent the perception otherwise. This one is much easier, for me personally. Can you see why those little box ticking exercises may be an issue though?

For every article there is in the paper about the figures being fiddled, someone should technically be dealt with via this legislation. Can a corporate tweet account be impartial? No because they are area focused and: Are they more likely to give help to a twitter follower they get on with, than to the chap waiting at the front counter, who is annoyed at watching them tweet?

And what about if two corporate tweet accounts have a discussion about which is best, north or south of the river Impartial? No. Activity. Yes. Public perception? Yes!

Or the corporate tweeters who openly refer to anonymous accounts as trolls? Impartial towards those exercising their human right to expression? No! Activity? Yes! Public perception? Yes!

Don't forget, we're two thirds through the schedule and not once has politics been mentioned. It broadly says any activity. ANY. Go as broad as you like. See what you can come up with.

"and in particular a member of a police force shall not take any active part in politics."

And so, at the very end, here we are. Politics.

Due to the existence of PCCs compliance with this is now an absolute impossibility. If I was to challenge an inappropriate policy, or say 'that was a good idea', then I would have breached this; technically, in either case. Of course if I do remain silent, that makes me either impolite or means I am failing to challenge, both of which put me in breach of the conduct regs of 2008.

You see, it's impossible. I don't think I can make the point better or really need to.

This outdated and contradictory legislation leaves me with a further question...does a PCC fall within the definition of 'member of a police force'? I'd suggest yes; as they will be leading police forces and they will by default have to be 'part of it'. I don't see how they could, technically, not be.

So, in a world which clearly requires impartial service from the police, of which PCCs, are now part: does this regulation not cancel their very existence? If it doesn't then the continued existence of this schedule is the biggest piece of hypocrisy I have ever come across.

This was an apolitical broadcast on behalf of no-one.

Reply From Home Office to Email to Nick Herbert 03/07/12:

"The proportion of officers on the front-line is increasing, crime is down, victim satisfaction is improving and the response to emergency calls is being maintained"

1st of August 2012

I am pleased to say that my crystal ball remains intact and fully functional:

"Dear Mr Patrick,

Thank you for your e-mail of 3 July to Nick Herbert about police resources. As I am sure you will appreciate, the Minister receives a lot of correspondence and is unable to respond to each item individually. Your e-mail has been passed to the Direct Communications Unit and I have been asked to reply.

In response to your comments on police funding, the Government has no choice but to deal with the deficit and that means that all public services must constrain their spending. As a service spending £14 billion a year, there is a broad consensus that the police can and must make their fair share of the savings that are needed. The Government is clear that savings need to be made while ensuring that the quality of service the public receive is maintained and, where possible, improved. This is not about salami-slicing policing but transformation and long-term change in the way services are delivered.

Nationally, around £2.1 billion of savings need to be made by the police service by 2015. Her Majesty's Inspectorate of Constabulary has challenged forces to drive through efficiencies and has shown that over half of the savings required nationally, £1.15 billion, can be achieved by forces just raising their performance to the average of their immediate peers. In addition, we know that there are other areas where savings can be made without affecting the level of service to the public. The police can, and are, making further savings by adopting an increasingly national approach to buying equipment and services, and forces can also make substantial savings in their IT spending.

In relation to your comments on police numbers, what matters is front-line services; how effective the police are at fighting crime. The effectiveness of a police force depends, not on overall numbers, but on how well it deploys its resources. As HMIC's latest report makes clear the front line of policing is being protected overall and service to the public has largely been maintained. The proportion of officers on the front-line is increasing, crime is down, victim satisfaction is improving and the response to emergency calls is being maintained. HMIC have also made clear that there is no simple link between officer numbers and crime levels, between numbers and the visibility of the police in the community, or between numbers and the quality of service provided.

No decisions have yet been taken on Tom Winsor's Final Report, but we have said that we think it provides a good basis for discussion and consultation, including through the formal police negotiating machinery. We remain committed to constructive engagement with the service throughout this process. We have entered into these discussions in good faith, and we have promised to listen to sensible and credible arguments made by the service."

The Silent Approach:

"Nothing has stopped, nothing has changed"

8th of August 2012

Back in 2010 something happened in my life that almost, very nearly, made me walk away from the career that I love; the oath that I am both proud and honoured to be sworn to.

This is not about what happened, these are stories for another time, when there are less pressing matters to be dealt with. This is however relevant, as during that time I began to look outside of the Police Service. This was long before I knew what I have shared with you all so far. Albeit that this was a temporary 'blip', I do still receive the odd, interesting email. One such email arrived only minutes ago. I have heard stories today of a think tank suggesting that the police train 'have a go heroes'. My training would consist quite simply of 'don't put yourself or anyone else in danger, call the police'.

Could you seriously imagine anyone suggesting 'have a go fire-fighters' or 'have a go surgeons'? This is a symptom of the lack of sense and understanding that surrounds the reform and debate agenda, when it comes to policing. It is, simply, policing for free.

To make matters worse we also have the drive for policing on the cheap, which leads me into the email:

"Dear James, Please forgive this generic email however I wanted to take this opportunity to make you aware that we are currently recruiting for a large number of Civilian Investigators in the Warwickshire Area. The Majority of work will fall within the Local Investigations remit based in either Nuneaton, Rugby or Leamington. Please see below for further details:

Main Purpose of the role:
Investigate offences of crime, and to actively participate in a wide range of evidence gathering and crime investigation tasks.

Main Responsibilities:
Actively identify and exploit investigative and intelligence opportunities in order to detect crime, highlighting those opportunities to staff and / or taking appropriate action.

Undertake tasks identified as being necessary in support of a criminal investigation, including seizure and viewing evidential material, taking evidential statements from victims and witnesses, undertaking house to house enquiries, undertaking property related enquiries, (this is not an exhaustive list of tasks).

Secure the best evidence thorough investigation and effective management of all available resources, working to an agreed case investigation plan, in order to detect crime and allow a considered decision to be taken regarding prosecution of offenders.

Prepare and submit complete evidential files to the Crown Prosecution Service observing the highest professional standards, and meeting the required Manual of Guidance in relation to quality & timeliness.

As required, attend court hearings and give evidence in relation to those aspects of any investigation which the post holder has had any involvement during the investigation process or are within their personal knowledge.

Liaise with internal units, other police forces and external agencies and the public, in relation to the gathering of evidence, identifying and tracing offenders and ensuring that all aspects of the investigation are taken into account.

Undertake sensitive high profile cases enquiries with limited supervision. Be familiar with and able to carry out any role within the Major Incident Room as described in the Major Incident Room Standard Administrative procedures.

Provide professional specialist advice and knowledge to all colleagues within the organisation in relation to all aspects of crime investigation and case file management. Commensurate with the use of 'designated powers' (Police Reform Act 2002).

Assist colleagues in crime matters, particularly where suspects have been arrested for like and possible linked offences. Act as liaison for officer for victims and witness of crime.

Undertake any relevant task at the discretion of the Detective Sergeant or Senior Investigating Officer, as deemed commensurate with the role.

Ensure integrity, fairness and consideration of the needs of others are incorporated into the daily duties and relationships with colleagues.

We look forward to speaking to you soon
Kind regards
G4S Policing Solutions"

As we spiral ever further towards a gloss over of the broader issues I have uncovered, courtesy of the Olympics, the economy and the apparently crumbling coalition...As we suffer further reality detached suggestions to put the public at risk, by cutting the police service budgets and officers and, now, by encouraging 'have a go policing'...As the way is paved, for the dangerous ground where vigilantism is one step away...As all of this happens:

The back door continues to open and, silently, the likes of G4S slip into crime investigation. Nothing has stopped, nothing has changed. More is at stake now, than ever before. If only the few are willing to stand, then so be it, but stand we will.

The Benefit of Education:

"the savage reductions in officer numbers continue to be clouded, in a whirlwind of horse dung"

9th of August 2012

It seems that common sense continues to fall by the way side and, that the true figures of the savage reductions in officer numbers continue to be clouded, in a whirlwind of horse dung.

But, before I discuss that, the primary focus of this blog being to educate you on the truth about officer numbers, I must of course discuss education itself.

The entry requirement for police officers will now be three 'A' levels. Before I say anything further I would like to point out that: the chap who tried to stab me and some other officers having seriously injured someone (by which I mean maimed) didn't ask about my schooling. He was too busy trying to kill me and some other people.

Come to think of it nor have any of the thousands of people I've dealt with.

None of the victims, suspects, coroners, judges, suspects, colleagues, witnesses, councillors, charity workers, prostitutes, tinkers, tailors, soldiers or spies have given the faintest hint of caring. This is because suitability to serve the public is not about education. It's about soul. In fact, a short while ago on a train journey I was talking to a consultant psychologist and we devised, on a napkin, a structure of tests of personality and emotional intelligence that would effectively identify the exact characteristics of a good police officer.

In essence I'm saying that we need to test the entire service in this way, to build a profile of desirable characteristics for good police officers and, only then, implement an entrance exam which ensures only those showing these positive characteristics would be recruited. The result, better service for the public. Of course, if we want to keep it to just what's on paper, never find this out, we should just carry on down the 'A' level road.

And from talking about education, in a fashion, it is is now time to educate you...on officer numbers:

Did anyone else pick up the current officer numbers in Sir Hugh Orde's piece on the Police Federation web site? He gives an officer head count for England and Wales of 8,000 fewer than the last figure, of 134,001 given by the Home Office. Sir Hugh Orde's view can be found here: (**63**).

In this article he clearly says:

"We still have 126,000 cops out there, so this isn't airbrushing of policing"

I would hasten to remind you all that only a couple of years back we had 143,000 police officers. The latest figures say that a further 16,000 (I think it is 16,091) police officers will be going; in this round of cuts alone. That leaves 110,000 officers across the country, or if your prefer 518 people per officer.

We know forces are so short already that they are taking on contract investigators, now, to do the jobs of detectives that aren't there. And we know that agency fees apply to this. Speak to any recruitment agency, that normally incorporates a finders commission and administration charges, on top of the hourly rates. This type of contract work can only increase, in order to bolster the growing short falls.

This aside we need to consider the prevalence of 5 team shift patterns. Meaning that officers are pretty much divided into teams of five, working a "2 earlies, 2 lates, 2 nights" shift pattern. Of course this is most prevalent in response teams, those attending emergencies, who account for about 10% of the workforce.

(give or take).

For the purpose of this though, let's says that all of the 110,000 officers left work on a five team basis, 24 hours a day (they won't as it now costs ten percent more to have officers on duty in the evening and at night). This means, by about April 2013, one officer on duty will be serving over 2,500 people.

2590 to be precise, if the population is considered as 57 million.

So let's say 3% of people need the police, which is about right for victims of crime, just crime, that's 77 people out of 2590, needing, relying on, that one officer, during their shift. Say that the single officer can deal with 1 incident, an hour, in a 9 hour shift; properly and to the standard the public deserve. (Remember that one incident can often take multiple officers a full shift or even multiple shifts).

This means, in the perfect, one incident an hour world, that 89% of those who need police officers won't be able to have them. This means that 97.7% of the 2590 people, that the single officer is responsible for, during their shift, will be completely unprotected and may see no officer at all for their entire life. Not even in passing. Now, take into account that the 'savings' next year are expected to double (£500 million up from £250 million in London alone)...are you worried yet?

This simple truth is now yours to think on, the benefit of a little education that doesn't come on paper, at Level 3. Public safety is paramount and these numbers are just one reason I can't sit idly by and watch this happen.

The Cut of The Jib:

"a total Surprise to the Home Secretary and, lest we forget, all completely normal for the Culture Secretary"

12th of August 2012

There was, a few hundred years ago, a far classier version of the phrase "I like your style".

It was, so history says, originally used by pirates in the 17th century. The expression refers to the forward sail on most ships, the jib. The course and speed of a ship is determined by the cut of the ship's jib so, saying that you like the cut of someone's jib is a way of saying, I like the way you're heading.

On the 18th of July, I posted a blog entitled "The Truth of the Matter", in which I awarded the Melton Mowbray awards, for big porky pies. It would appear that my jib was cut in the right direction, even then. I said, that there was no way that the G4S farce was a surprise on the 11th of July (the day after the story broke into the mainstream at lunchtime). Don't forget, we already knew, eight days before that, that the military had taken over checkpoint security.

But no, nobody knew. Despite their weekly meetings, nobody knew. Despite it even being in the main Olympic Board minutes back as far as May, nobody knew. Despite eventual admissions that they knew at the end of June, having initially said 11th July: nobody knew.

They knew alright. The 11th of July (or "d'you lie" if you want to get phonetic) was just a forced sell by date. They got caught out, plain and simple.

Now, before we recap, I must make two observations on human nature:
1) Lies are not sustainable within a group, because self preservation always takes over. And;
2) If you want to make an admission of a lie, it's best to do it quietly and while people are distracted.

This weekend, Theresa May was speaking to John Sopel on the BBC, a day shy of the Olympics closing ceremony. She made a completely innocuous statement that the Military were always going to run the Olympic security. We know this. The issue was the additional deployment of thousands more troops to bolster the G4S failure. This is actually quite a nice gloss over, under the old lie within the truth rule. Where were you looking when she said this? At the Olympics or the other, most shocking and upsetting headlines?

I remember quite clearly that when she first admitted knowing back in June, she did so just after the verdict on the sad case of Ian Tomlinson, had been reported. Where were you looking then? In fact, in her letter to the HASC, she says an awful lot about how much they knew (and interestingly shows how many hooks G4S have in public services too): (**64**)

I see a most curious pattern developing here. Thankfully, we live in modern times; so here is an ITN video of Mrs May, on the 12th of July, making her position quite clear: (**65**). Her nose was growing, even then. And, to prove my point about Human Nature, here she is on the 16th of July, ensuring we all think G4S are the puppet sons of an Italian carpenter: (**66**).

Of course, the good old Defence Secretary, Phillip Hammond helps when it comes to unravelling all this. On the 16th July the BBC quote him as saying:
    "he had authorised the deployment of the 3,500 military personnel, bringing the total number of military personnel - from three services and including reservists - contributing to Games security to 17,000."
And then:
    "Mr Hammond later told the defence select committee that the deployment request had come "as no great surprise".

He told MPs it became clear that some extra servicemen would be needed two weeks ago when the beginning of the lock-down at the park started. He said the servicemen had their "notice to move" reduced at the weekend, which informed them of imminent deployment. All of the extra servicemen had been on standby for such a contingency". So, it was no great surprise to the Defence Secretary but a total Surprise to the Home Secretary and, lest we forget, all completely normal for the Culture Secretary, Jeremy Hunt.

What I find most curious is Hammond's statement about contingencies, the main reason being this article from the Guardian yesterday: (**67**). In it, the other party who didn't know anything was wrong, the police chiefs, admit they knew it was wrong at the beginning of the year, but explicitly say there was no contingency button:

"The group expressed concern that there was no independent regulator of G4S, which meant its progress in meeting targets leading up to the Games had gone largely unmonitored until it was almost too late to take action. It meant there was nobody who could press a panic button".

Well, this statement came from the Olympic Security Group, who had overall responsibility to coordinate security via all agencies and report to the main Olympics Board. Who did they think was doing the regulating?? Of course, they go on:

"It acknowledged that there had been warnings that G4S would not be able to deliver on its promises since the beginning of the year".

See, that's not the 11th of July is it.

Of course, there is also this article from the 15th of July, in which Lord Coe, Jeremy Hunt and Theresa May, all say everything's fine...but of course we discover they knew as far back as September 2011 that it wasn't.

But then they seek absolution by claiming the Home Office weren't informed by the Security Group:

"Home Office ministers were warned about security issues surrounding the Games 10 months ago. HM Inspectorate of Constabulary raised its concerns in a confidential report in September 2011 after a number of inspections to test that the security plans of Locog, the Games organising committee, were on track. The Home Office said HMIC had not carried out an investigation into G4S, and the issues flagged by HMIC had all been dealt with by February.

On Friday the home secretary, Theresa May, told the Commons she learned of the security shortfall only this last week. Reports that the security minister James Brokenshire attended daily senior-level Olympics security meetings were incorrect, the Home Office said. A spokesman said the meetings with department officials, G4S and LOCOG over the past three weeks were not focused on the G4S recruiting problems".

What I see here is a pattern of "it's not my fault". News flash: It is all of your faults collectively.

As a final link, and this is homework for you, here is the correspondence so far from and to the Home Affairs Select Committee, relating to this farce: (**68**). I am glad in many ways that people were so quick to jump to their responses. They are now committed to those lines. Any changes of direction mean only one thing. For this reason, because it points in the same direction as the tide I'm chasing: I like the cut of this jib.

The Return on Investment:

"For every £1 I put in, I had bought £235 worth of influence over government decision making"

19th of August 2012

I make you all a promise.

Aside from in this sentence, I will not be mentioning the rather crass, "four horsemen of the apocalypse" comment, made by Blair Gibbs. I make no promises about my prolific use of commas or semicolons. And yes; I do use them like hundreds and thousands.

Last night, I was having the most amazing, vivid dream. I find often, that my unconscious helps me unravel large amounts of information and, I'm happy for it to do so. That's what it does for a living. This morning I awoke to a very simple answer, to a complex mess, that has been perturbing me. Is there a way to look at think tanks, such as Policy Exchange and encapsulate, in simple form, the concerning nature of the influence they wield? It would seem that my unconscious has done the job for me, in a way that everyone should be able to understand my complex concerns, about lobbying and influence.

Take £1 from your pocket, go to any bank and ask them for an account that will provide an annualised return of 23400%. I guarantee you would be laughed at or chased out with a pitchfork; or that the police would be called, as they would suspect you were an armed robber using code.

Well, there is one place this happens: Policy Exchange. Now, before anyone says it, I am aware that they have worked on this for years so the return may be less (or even more), but this is the basic explanation. In short, it's the concept which is important.

Last year Policy Exchange took in donations, to the 'charity', to the tune of £1.5 million, out of a total income of about £2.1 million. Quite the majority you could say.

(On the original blog I made an error and said it was £1.7 million – for the sake of not redoing the maths, the figures are based on the higher figure originally used).

As I've covered previously, Restricted Funds can only be used for specified purposes, so by default, in this case, must be directed towards certain kinds of research and resultant, policy papers.

Let's be fair and say only a quarter went to the Crime and Justice department: that would be £425,000. Let's imagine that this was the amount that went into the research and policy papers of the successful PCC policy, which came directly out of Policy Exchange. We now know that the Government Are putting around £100 million into PCCs.

Effectively, if I had put the whole £425,000 into Policy Exchange restricted funds, directed specifically at researching and producing papers on PCCs...as it became a successful policy, implemented by government: for every £1 I put in, I had bought £235 worth of influence over government decision making.

If we looked at this as ROI it would be 23400%, the very figure that would have had the average person laughed out of the bank, or arrested.

It seems that £1 can punch well above weight. As long as it goes through the right mechanism. We've had the banking scandal, we've had the phone hacking scandal. I think we are on the cusp of the biggest parliamentary scandal in history. The mechanism of the think tanks, the extent of their influence...this 'ROI' should be of significant concern to us all. When £1 buys £234 more, in influence over parliament, it tells us that the last days of Rome are about to repeat themselves. It is said that society and democracy can live, successfully, for no more than 200 years.

I've checked and we are several years overdue.

The problem for the average person on the street is this:
An independent office was implemented, by design not bound to politics, so that corruption and crime at all levels could be dealt with. That was the Office of Constable. Very soon it will be directly overseen by political figures, with power to stop or encourage investigations.

When we are faced with an ROI in politics of 23400%...what do you think that decision will invariably be?

The Responsibility of Power:

"Haste causes problems. Haste with power causes damage.   Power without responsibility is just plain terrifying"

22nd of August 2012

One of my favourite quotes, from a comic book superhero, comes from Nightwing:

"You're not too big to be spanked".

This is a sound principle to remember.

A second comic book quote comes from the Hollywood adaptation of Spiderman. (Never my favourite, even though I used to have the costume as a child):

"With great power, comes great responsibility".

Even though it hurts me to say it, this fromage is both pertinent and relevant.

Yesterday I tweeted out two topics for debate...and debated they were. The first was this:

"Taking into account Policy Exchange's influential nature; do their actions have direct sway on public interest?"

The answer was a resounding 'yes'.

Policy Exchange, as I've said repeatedly, are proud of the depth of their influence, PCCs being one success for them (clearly affecting public interest without the public finding it interesting). This was backed up by a recent BBC article on social housing. (**70**). The best point made on this, which really ended the debate with an exclamation mark, was that:

This isn't painted as a government policy backed by Policy Exchange research; it's painted as Policy Exchange policy, backed by Downing Street.

Aside from scaring the bejesus out of me, this tells us that they do have direct sway over government. Ergo, they have direct sway over the public interest.

With that power, comes great responsibility and, as we know there are open questions about lobbying, we should be at least interested in how seriously that is being taken. No one needs reminding that these people are unelected. Yet, they are now touching our lives with the power of those who have been subject to democratic election. For me, this draws a new boundary. Should we now consider, by virtue of this influence and responsibility, the effect on public interest, that Policy Exchange have evolved into a pseudo public office?

I looked to the Attorney General for guidance and believe the answer is yes.

The AG defines a public office as:
"an office of trust concerning the public, ...by

whomever and in whatever way the officer is appointed".
This includes voluntary functions by the way. Such as charities.

Does the work of Policy Exchange concern the public? Without doubt. Is it an office of trust? If they are producing policy which is directly steering government decisions, then the answer is also yes. They are self appointed in this position of influence, so, yes, it all seems to fit the bill.

The AG goes on to say:
"A public office holder is an officer who discharges any duty in the discharge of which the public are interested".
Are the public interested in how they are housed and policed? Of course!

Duty? In its broader sense, yes to that too. Policy Exchange carry out activity which results in decisions on the future of the public.

The AG keeps the definition of public office purposefully loose and, because of that, I'm quite happy to state that Policy Exchange have voluntarily stepped into the scope of that broad definition. Of course the side effect of that is new exposure, to the common law offence of

Misconduct in a Public Office. I reference Spiderman once more:

"With great power comes great responsibility".

This also leads me on to the second topic of yesterday; a discussion point more than anything. Promotion opportunities have been frozen for serving police officers who have passed the relevant, national examinations. This is because supervision levels are being dropped and remodelled. In the same breath, 150 graduates are being recruited on a scheme that will see then go from PC to Inspector in 36 months.

The debate was fierce around education and selection and was interesting to watch. I've previously spoken of the need to study police officers and use that to build a new recruitment and promotion process; I won't repeat it or link to it here. The main point, for me is two-fold.

Firstly, the management decision that led to this raises a serious question, over the valuing of staff, at a time when morale in the service is at its lowest ebb. This kind of duplicitous, mixed message can only lead to the current officers feeling not good enough. And could lead to a less than desirable feeling of elitism among the new recruits. In essence, through poor judgement, the current 'management' have said to current officers, "there is promotion, just not for you".

The unintended consequence of the poor management decision will also have an impact on how 'fast track' applicants are treated by peers. In the workplace this will cause division and two way resentment that will be retained as ranks are climbed. This is a well studied aspect of human psychology and simply cannot be dismissed or ignored.

In short, a responsibility to look after both existing and new staff has been failed, by default, by those with power to make decisions. This may sound a harsh assessment but think it through, logically.

I have heard the impact that this has had already, by the issue being allowed to bubble under the surface. Subsequently I chose to facilitate the venting of this, rather than leave the pressure cooker on. That was within my power and the responsibility needed taking. I worry about the culture this may develop and how this may ultimately impact in the way we do what we promise to do: serve the public. For me, that is above all else.

Secondly, there is the question of experience. Are people ready, with three years as a police officer, to make life or death decisions, relating not just to one incident, but multiple incidents, thousands of people, hundreds of officers? Take into account that in 36 months, they will have been a Constable, Sergeant and Inspector, will they have a full grasp of the intricacies and pitfalls of each role? I can't answer that question, because it is down to the individual and, I don't generalise.

But, my gut feeling, my instinct for danger and potential trouble, which is an accurate gauge, is telling me to beware. I'm just not sure the weight of responsibility can sink in if you are forced to butterfly, especially if a work based assessment model, forcing action to tick boxes, is followed.

Haste causes problems. Haste with power causes damage. Power without responsibility is just plain terrifying. Thankfully, there is nothing wrong with raising concerns, it's good to talk. It's a responsible use of what power you have; as they say, evil can only triumph when good men remain silent and do nothing. And, sometimes, just sometimes, where people with real power are concerned, they need to be reminded to use it well and with forethought.

To be responsible with it in every way.

I began with a good principle and shall end
with the same: You're never too big to be
spanked.

The Modest Proposal:

28th of August 2012

In the 18th century, the rather wonderful
Jonathan Swift wrote the satire, 'A Modest
Proposal', in which he encouraged that children
become a source of both food and income, to
solve the woes of Ireland's poor. I present to
you a modest proposal of my own...

yammering of the poor and utterly feeble 'middle' classes, the detail of my meeting with the Home Secretary has been struck from the record, to avoid any unpleasantries.

Nor shall you find me standing fixed in any county, for I have chosen to stand broadly, to represent the dedicated voters, wherever the turnout is likely to be lowest; as the dreary, dark of November sets in, I could be standing in your own shire and you would not know until I slunk out of the dark, grasping you lightly by the shoulder and pressing the sharp blade of persuasion into your side; whispering as softly as a leafless, winter tree: "vote for me".

I will wait for you, as the visible representation of your conscience, glinting in the light of the doorway, as you cast your ballot and return home; ever under my watchful eye. I will do this because the first part of my modest proposal is that, for your good, the balances should be tipped in my favour, in the favour of the greater good I represent, from the outset.

I propose to carry this out personally, until the expected 18% of you, have seen fit to accept my sharp and cutting powers of persuasion. Of course there shall be vetting at the door too, built in as part of this process. It is essential that those who would later seek to make noise have their concerns quelled from the outset, lest they become 'difficult' thereafter.

The necessary capacity for this will be provided, by the temporary installation of a power-grid connected incinerator. Thus, as my incisive blade gives weight to the voting decisions of the wealthy, the poor and less desirable shall provide heat and light, to the subsequent debates, in a much less troublesome and quieter manner.

Being an educated and respected man, known amidst some of the shadier corridors, I have mooted this proposition be replicated across our fair land. I am nothing if not an advocate of regional equality. Needless to say, in the poorer north and in Wales, the incinerators will burn more fiercely - as should be expected where a higher percentage of 'fuel' is to be found.

With much vintage Cognac and quiet seating at the, more refined, gentleman's clubs I have managed to be convinced of the full support of the political might of Oxford and Cambridge; they quite literally are steeped in the white stuff: just what is needed to get the job done. And, as the persuaded electorate has the overwhelming vote counted, while the electric light burns brighter and more cheaply than ever, I shall turn my attentions away from the twinkling reflections of chandeliers and towards the resolution of crime and disorder, the repugnant afflictions that blight our image across the former empire.

Being a reasonable and balanced man I have invested heavily in research, to reinforce my proposals. Research that spews forth unquestioning support for my modest proposal. The think tankers have been most kind, as has the towering, financial might of the East India Trading Company, my primary brethren in this total crusade against the criminal and, most vocal, classes.

My research, the independent research I commissioned, suggests that once elected I should immediately dispense with the services of all but five warranted constables. They are best suited to be kept in boxes, mouths bound with gaffer tape lest their legal services be required.

Only a chief shall remain, trussed as a pig, to squeal at my beck and call, by virtue of a filled trough in the yard of my newly constructed police 'mansion centre'. Should they squeal too often or be distracted from the trough for more than a minute, they shall be expelled with some violence and turned into fertiliser for the flower beds, which in turn will feed the honey production of the bees, taken from the hives at the former NPIA.

This honey shall be jarred and sold by the covert enforcement department, the WI, who will act as my Stasi; watchful eyes ever on those of 'middle class' with ideals of upward social mobility. There is no subversion so dangerous, as that of a commoner with upwards momentum and a cake recipe beyond their standing.

With the chiefs in troughs and the constables back in the boxes they have constantly bemoaned were empty, the East India Trading Company will bring forth their armies of lower than minimum wage patrols, rescued from humble beginnings, as small children, across the known world. I promise you this, none younger than 12 years of age shall don the bright red coats of the neighbourhood trooper, operating under powers, newly devolved from the Home Secretary.

Each shall busy themselves in sifting the rubbish bins of our fair residents, using the

'Deregulation of Investigation Act', to watch for signs of elaborate purchases from Elizabeth Duke, which may indicate excessive income. Income from possible crime subject to immediate confiscation.

It is estimated under the East India arrangement, that a troop of 5,000 can be provided at a beguilingly small cost of 25 pence per year. This may seem an outlandish claim; however, once the poor are ejected from social housing into the new, communal camp, in the port town of Liverpool and, once the great wall around it is finished, by the hands of those retired on a public sector pension prior to 60 year of age; there will be plenty of housing standing empty.

Subsequently troopers will be housed for free, becoming the community they serve, the big society; they will fend for themselves via extended use of powers to issue tickets under the Proceeds of Possible Crime Act. In short, this act provides the ability to derive immediate income where it is thought a crime might have, possibly, occurred. This will be judged on the standards of the East India Board and agreed quarterly.

In essence they, the troopers, shall be self

sufficient via the use of penalties to be paid on the spot, which they shall return each day with a 90% commission to be paid to me, as PCC. I will then deduct 60% of this as a local tax and pay the remainder to the East India Trading Company.

For the first time, the provision of policing will be self sufficient; in fact it shall make money. If only Peel had been as visionary.

Once the housing handover is complete, power supplies may be disconnected to all but the most lush of premises, or those willing to buy East India Electricity Tokens and, the surrounding land, once used for those most disdain-able 'skate parks' will become agricultural once more. The Land Army of middle class wives and children, with enlistment enforced by the newly formed River Cottage Brigade, shall tend to the nation's needs for food and livestock, negating the need for expensive education for the masses, as they busy themselves; the men shall be set to work, rebuilding the industry of the nation under watchful eyes of selected Lords and East India subsidiaries.

There will, by account of my proposal, be no time for criminality, with the introduction of

National Standard Working Time, being from 4am until 8pm. Any repeated shirking or attempted 'sickness' will result in a bus ride to the banks of the Liver.

Liverpool shall be left to its own devices, secured by a guard of newly retired soldiers, so affected by PTSD that they will not recognise their own countrymen in squalor. As such the whole mess within, as is the natural order of things, shall fizzle itself out within a few months and without a recountable fuss to concern the dear wives of the gentry.

This proposal, aside from also reducing the burden of mass education has certain other benefits:
The blights of extended runways will cease to be a problem, as the ghastly low cost airlines, cease to export the low rent, for brief periods of international disgrace.

The NHS will no longer be required as the Land Army's skills with livestock will, eventually, provide enough knowledge to deliver basic midwifery or utilise the bolt gun in cases of illness requiring more detailed attention. The shibboleth of medicine being removed will be as a weight lifted from the neck of society. Lady luck, with a zero cost implication, will take her place as the head of natural selection.

All of this shall be achieved under the loosely worded oath of mine, as your PCC, and for transparency, my oath will be repeated daily on all broadcast channels, at fifteen minute intervals throughout the day. A constant reminder.

Of course, finally, my proposal need not be unduly hindered by any change in national government and the reasons for this are two fold.

Firstly, elections will always be held on the national days of extended work, which herald a mass effort of 72 hours of solid work, without rest, to showcase our annual triumphs to visiting, aspiring leaders from across the world. Secondly, by establishment, the PCC is now statute and cannot be undone, so should the central government, to which I am in no way affiliated - and there is no evidence of any conversation as you may recall - fail: any new government would have to direct a change in law. This is coped with by virtue of passage through the House of Lords, each of which will have acquired land and, East India Company patronage, of a shire under the new regime and, by virtue of my oft repeated oath: with which I would encourage the investigation of any new politicians, by my troopers, for such historic or current misdemeanour's as I see fit.

Thus, to paraphrase, enough muck would be slung, to maintain the success, of each of the elements of this proposal, across the board. I hope the security by design and, ultimate longevity of this modest proposal, to permanently eliminate criminality and drive improvements in our society, through effective use of the police, are of interest to you. I continue to lobby, a select and choice few and, I look forward to grasping your shoulder on a cold, dark night in November; as we herald in the new era together.

I seek not your approval, but your cooperation and woe betide that the opportunity, to improve our fair land, be missed, through choice.

The Futility of Surrender:

"Parliament will finally exempt itself from the law"

30th of August 2012

Herodotus told a good yarn.

In 'The Histories' he sets out to document his present, in order that it can be preserved for the future. He calls this an inquiry or investigation. I hadn't read his work at all until very recently, yet found myself feeling a weird sense of home.

Standing out for me, taking into account the challenges surrounding the future of the vocation that called to me, is the following passage:

"Thrasybulus was an ally of Periander, the tyrant of Corinth. Periander asks Thrasybulus for advice on ruling. Instead of responding, he takes the messenger for a walk in a field of wheat, where he proceeds to cut off all of the best and tallest ears of wheat. The message, correctly interpreted by Periander, was that a wise ruler would pre-empt challenges to his rule by "removing" those prominent men who might be powerful enough to challenge him"

The Police, some of the police, are the tall corn and, slowly: by push, pull, snap or crush, the field is being levelled.

When the brave and decent few can no longer stand, independent of government, against corruption; when they are so few that they have no choice to but to deal with local crime and civil disorder only; while private companies do the bulk for profit; when PCCs can stop and encourage investigations by virtue of their oath: parliament will finally exempt itself from the law.

I fear for the future, this bleak and stage managed future; but that shall not override my will to act in the present. So, once again, time to shine a light...

By virtue of the fact I have stood up, I have recently been told two things about think tanks, direct from the mouths of people in the know:
   "Think Tanks often have an MP or Lord in their ranks, sometimes in unpaid roles, sometimes fully paid. Other think tanks just sponsor Parliamentary Groups related to their work, giving them unfettered access to MPs. Aside from that, think tanks make contributions to committees and generate research for individual MPs to back up issues they raise in the Commons. The best resourced think tanks just keep key legislators in their pockets. Like, IDS (Iain Duncan Smith) and the Centre for Social Justice".

There is more from a second source:

"The Relationship between think tanks and minister is cosy - they are basically mates and they talk. Sometime the "research" is a testing ground for the general popularity of a policy, sometimes it is a justification for implementing a less popular policy. That's why think tanks go in and out of popularity depending on who's in power. Think tanks have to have a commercial backer so, results will generally be favourable to that backer, it is a good investment. It's a shady world, but there is no 'real' concept of direct payment, it's much more insidious".

These are credible people, within this world and; I find the fact that is widely known about quite terrifying indeed. If only because it confirms everything I believed already. I did however think it best to cross reference this, against old material. This checks out with everything I have put together so far.

As a final measure though I had to follow upon the IDS information, to verify the veracity and back up what was being said about 'legislators being in pockets'.

Mr Smith is the Chairman of the Centre For Social Justice and during the foreword, that he wrote for it, keeps making reference to 'us' when referring to reports that the centre has completed. This is the entry for the Centre in Wikipedia, which confirms it was set up by IDS and states it has cross party representation. (**70**).

It clearly does have this and MP's from all parties are members. The entry also contains a list of the policies that the Centre have reported on, including Police and Prison Reform, Education, Mental Health to name a few.
In a March 2009 presentation in Ottawa, Tim Montgomerie and Matthew Elliott described the Centre for Social Justice as part of the infrastructure of the conservative movement in Britain. Quite large and very 'think tanky' is this infrastructure. The following slides were produced and delivered as part of a conference to show the growth of conservatism in Britain. These are on the website Conservative Home blogs. (**71**).

They show the conservative movement in 1997 and then again in 2009. There are many common names in the 2009 slide that have had a direct impact on current policies.

Tim Montgomerie was Iain Duncan Smith's chief of staff for his last two months as Conservative leader and in 2004 helped him to establish the Centre for Social Justice. Montgomerie also launched the Conservative

Home website in 2005.

Another interesting link from their site relates to a vote in 2010. It states that:

"Over the last few days Conservative Home has been surveying readers and 'influentials' about the quality of the London think tanks. Tomorrow we'll publish how readers voted. Today we publish the results of voting by 94 influential journalists, parliamentarians, bloggers and other thought-leaders".

The Centre for Social justice was voted the think tank that has had the biggest influence on the Cameron project: The CSJ only just beat Policy Exchange. The CSJ won 40 votes and PX won 36 votes. Third, a long way behind, was Respublica with 5 votes.

The CSJ has played a leading role in David Cameron's biggest idea, "the Big Society". Seventy CSJ policy ideas have been adopted by the Conservative Party. Policy Exchange was voted the think tank that was most effective overall: Won 33 votes. The CSJ won 29 votes. The Tax Payers' Alliance won 18 votes. PX's most recent success was its publication arguing against NI rises.

The Tax Payers' Alliance was voted the think tank likely to cause most difficulty for any

Conservative government, Winning a massive 55 of the votes in this section. Next came Reform with 10 votes and then the Centre for Policy Studies with 8 votes. The TPA recently produced a manifesto that set it against key parts of the Conservative programme. The Left's argument that it is a Tory front organisation is not believed by our panel of influentials.

The Adam Smith Institute was voted the think tank best at developing new talent: The ASI won 18 votes. Policy Exchange won 16 votes. The Tax Payers' Alliance and the CSJ both won 14 votes. Again, the link for this document is here: (**72**).

An entry relating to the Centre For Social Justice in Powerbase states:

"The Centre for Social Justice says it is an independent think tank established by Rt Hon Iain Duncan Smith MP in 2004, to seek effective solutions to the poverty that blight parts of Britain".

In a March 2009 presentation Tim Montgomerie and Matthew Elliott described the Centre for Social Justice as part of the infrastructure of the conservative movement in Britain. In 2011 Montgomerie wrote,'the old right wing think tanks weren't particularly helpful to the Tory modernisers and so they built their own. ... The Centre for Social Justice gave Iain Duncan Smith his poverty-fighting plans.'

In 2009 Iain Duncan Smith delivered a speech to the Heritage Foundation in Washington, thanking them for their help in 'building up an international network of individuals and think tanks interested in centre right approaches to the delivery of social justice'.

In 2010 the Centre for Social Justice was voted the think tank which has most influence on the Cameron Project by Conservative Home website and every MP who has taken part in the Centre's 'Inner City Challenge' is a member of the Conservative Party. The list includes Andrew Selons, David Burrowes, John Penrose, Patrick Mercer and Rt Hon Oliver Letwin. The link is here: (73).

Tim Montgomerie set up a group in 1990 called the Conservative Christian Fellowship. This attracted 40 Conservative party members. He is very anti gay and was vocal with it. The group tried to strip Tony Blair's new labour of the fact that they were Christian. Anyway, in 2000, William Hague set up a 'Renewing One Nation' task force to shadow Labour's Social Exclusion

Unit. The group was mainly funded by Stanley Kalmsand, Tim Montgomerie was selected to be the groups national director. When the task force was set up Montgomerie argued that 'The Conservative Party has not done enough to show that it cares about the same problems that they [Labour] do. We need to use a different language on some issues and we need to do a lot more policy thinking.'

Now, the funder of that 'Renewing One Nation' Stanley Kalms, born 21 November 1931, is the former treasurer of The Conservative Party. He was the Director of the Centre for Policy Studies think tank from 1991-2001. Kalms is the life president and former chairman of DSG International (formerly Dixons Group). DSG owns Dixons.com, Currys, The Link and PC World outlets. He spent his entire career from 1948 working for Dixons, which was founded by his father Charles Kalms in 1937.

Kalms provided £300,000 funding for Tim Montgomerie to establish the Renewing One Nation group within the Conservative Party. The funding was provided on the condition that the organisation be non-denominational. Renewing One Nation was a predecessor to the Centre for Social Justice and claimed that the Conservative Party's proposed tax cuts would 'foster a compassionate society where people are rewarded for taking responsibility for themselves, their families and their communities.'

On 28 March 2005 Montgomerie set up the Conservative Home blog in an attempt to 'combine the concepts of a think-tank and online newspaper and its aim is to provide a forum for the revival of Conservative thinking and policies'.

Conservative Party Francis Maude sent Montgomerie to Washington in 2006 to help develop an online campaign strategy similar to the US campaigns that had successfully discredited John Kerry's Democratic hopes in 2004. Montgomerie argued that the Conservative Home blog could be used to tackle the 'left-wing bias' of the BBC.
This can all be found on these links here: (**74** & **75**).

Just quickly, do you remember those slides about Conservatism presented in in March 2009 in Canada?

These are from IDS' members register entries: 8 - 13 March 2009, to Washington and Canada, to attend a conference run by the Institute of

Marriage and Family Canada (IMFC) and give evidence to a select committee of the Canadian House of Commons. My flights and accommodation in Canada were paid by the IMFC and my accommodation in Washington by the Centre for Social Justice. (Registered 21 March 2009)

and;

24-30 September 2005, to USA accompanied by my wife, to attend a conference on social justice arranged jointly by the Centre for Social Justice and the Heritage Foundation. Our travel and accommodation during the conference was paid for by the Centre for Social Justice of which I am an unremunerated director. (Registered 17 October 2005)

He also received an honorary membership of The Bucks Club:
Name of donor: Buck's Club 1919
Address of donor : 18 Clifford Street, London W15 3RF
Amount of donation or nature and value if donation in kind: honorary membership; value £1,300 per annum
Date of receipt of donation: January 2010
Date of acceptance of donation: January 2010
Donor status: private members' club

(Registered 6 September 2010)
All of this can be found on this brilliant
interface tool: (**76**).

In short...this all seems to confirm that key
legislators are indeed directly in the pocket of
think tanks...just as my sources say. Is this
ethical? Compatible with the Ministerial Code?
Legal even? There is more to this, I have no
doubt and: the truth will out, as long at the tall
corn is not completely destroyed.

...for now, I look to another, more caustic voice
from the past, Horace, to put the right words in
my mouth:
   "It is courage, courage, courage, that raises
the blood of life to crimson splendour. Live
bravely and present a brave front to adversity".

I choose not to bow to the sense of futility that
laps at my heels and wakes me up in the night. I
choose not to surrender. Such is my lot.

The Last Good Reason:

3rd of September

pressed up against my back; her head resting on my neck as we talk. We smile. We laugh.

She has a soft laugh. I stop, we walk, we kiss. We sit on a bench; "budge up" she says. I budge up. We kiss.

grave. She took an overdose. In the end, the only people who were looking for Emma that night were the police. She hadn't committed any offences, she hadn't been a victim of crime; yet it was the police who were looking. There was no one else.

The Blazing Saddles of the Apocalypse:

"Pat Garrett keeps ringing for me from ACPO head office, wants a meeting or something"

10th of September 2012

William H. Bonney (a.k.a. McCarty) was born around the 23rd of November, 1859. He was better known as Billy the Kid.

According to the legend that grew around him, he killed 21 men. He was famed as a 19th-century gunman who participated in the Lincoln County War:
The Kid was a deputised 'regulator', who fought, with others, against a corrupt sheriff, deep in the pockets of a private industry magnate, who was trying to maintain monopoly on the beef industry. This went awry and The Kid became a frontier outlaw in the Wild West.

Robin Hood was a heroic character in our own folklore.

He always appears as a highly skilled archer and swordsman, best known for "robbing from the rich and giving to the poor". He was assisted, according to the legend, by a group of fellow outlaws known as his "Merry Men". His constant enemy was the reputedly corrupt Sheriff of Nottingham, who sought to further his own status and position. In the earliest sources, Robin Hood was described as a Yeoman, which has many meanings, including "one who carries out various duties for the sovereign as assigned to his office".

Billy the Kid and Robin Hood seem to have a bit in common, they had an office and ended up on the wrong side of it; both had problems with the Sheriff and: there were horses everywhere.

Today PCCs are having a jamboree. A good old sit around the camp fire where, I imagine, beans are being eaten and songs sung. Outside the venue, tethered up, are some horses, belonging to two of the self proclaimed 'horsemen of the apocalypse'.

It's a good job they are there, it is after all their research that gave us PCCs, a measure so unpopular it led Nick Herbert to finally throw his teddy and, leave the government because Number 10 did 'F all'. The two apocalyptic cow-pokes are there, to teach PCCs about 'policing in austere times'. Now that's reassuring, it will all be alright then.

Thankfully, I'm realising, some PCC candidates actually understand either policing itself, or the value of public service. I don't support any of them but, to speak to, some are actually quite nice; you can see this from Twitter. What I hope is, that all of them have have the good sense to listen to police officers about the job they know; rather than the writers of research which is created to support, frankly rubbish, government policy. In short, let's not be saddled with nonsense.

Meanwhile (and on that topic) I hear rumblings that the pervasively silent ACPO have something to say...possibly as brilliant as the inspiring words, of the lead on 'rewards and recognition' last week...yep, you guessed it pardners:

It might be that coppers should never speak to PCCs...about anything. (The ACPO guidelines are published on their website, 13.3 is a good one).

I can't help but wonder if this is because chiefs will be able to be sacked by PCCs. I mean...what could a 'policeman-officer' possibly tell a PCC that may cause a chief to be questioned over decision making and performance?

I wish the PCCs well, all of them and, maybe, unless ACPO turn me into an outlaw for saying that:
This could actually turn out quite well. The choice lies with them...the PCC candidates. Either they will change the well established, legendary view that Sheriffs are naughty

or...this is set to be an even more outrageous remake of Blazing Saddles.

Now...someone called Pat Garrett keeps ringing for me from ACPO head office, wants a meeting or something.

Saddle up deputies. Yee-Ha!

The Wolf At The Gate:

24th of September 2012

launched a foul-mouthed tirade at officers who stopped him riding his bicycle out of the main Downing Street gates. The MP reiterated his regret when he ventured in front of cameras for the first time on Monday morning. However, he pointedly refused to answer questions about whether he had branded the police "plebs" - as their leaked written records of the exchange suggest. In the letter, Sir Jeremy revealed that the head of security at Number 10 and the Prime Minister's principal private secretary Chris Martin had spoken to the police sergeant involved."

"The Prime Minister spoke to Andrew Mitchell and made very clear that his behaviour fell short of what he expects of his ministers. (Mr Mitchell) then phoned the police officer in question to apologise personally and he has since reiterated his apology in public. The officer has accepted his apology," the mandarin wrote. Sir Jeremy went on: "I have subsequently discussed the matter with the Metropolitan Police Commissioner, Bernard Hogan-Howe. Like the Prime Minister he is obviously very disappointed at the lack of respect shown towards the police and agrees that the behaviour fell short of what the police should expect, in particular from members of the Government. However, in light of the apology given, and also the fact that the officer concerned has accepted the apology and does not wish to pursue the matter further, the Metropolitan Commissioner reiterated that no further action would be taken."

See...big hoo-ha. Nothing doing.

So, beyond stating the obvious...

That worse has been said, about our mum's;
That the use of the word pleb is a new one on 99.9% of all coppers
and;
That if someone thinks a police officer is a pleb...then what does that person think of those who generally need us most?

...there really is nothing much else to say.

Except that it's important to get some perspective beyond this kerfuffle, to look at the man involved; just out of curiosity.

Blimey.

However, I'm not one to be swayed by an opinion alone, so here is what I have learned about the Chief Whip, the minister in charge of discipline.

at the centre of a tax avoidance case. He paid money into DV3 Ltd, a subsidiary of which used a legal loophole in 2006 to avoid paying £2.6 million in stamp duty on the purchase of a commercial property in London, The Times reported. Although the transaction was legal, HM Revenue and Customs has described it as "aggressive tax avoidance" – a practice Chancellor George Osborne has pledged to clamp down on."

I then found this from 29 September 2011:

"In an unprecedented attack Human Rights Watch has accused cabinet minister Andrew Mitchell of being 'disingenuous' and 'misleading' in an interview about the misuse of aid in Ethiopia. The leading, international NGO suggests the UK has bowed to pressure from the Ethiopian government allowing it to dictate the terms on which British taxpayers' money is monitored.

Last month the Bureau of Investigative Journalism and BBC Newsnight exposed how long-term development aid was being used for political purposes by the Ethiopian government, effectively starving the opposition into submission. Interviewed on Newsnight last Wednesday by Jeremy Paxman, Mr Mitchell, the international development secretary, asserted that no British development support goes through the government of Ethiopia. He also stated officials had conducted an on-the-ground investigation and found no evidence of the systemic misuse of food aid".

Read the rest here if you like: (**80**). In fact, you can fill your boots and read a blog regarding the Newsnight performance here: (**81**). By the time I got to this...(**82**)...and read the phrase 'desk based investigations' I stopped reading and went for a cigarette.

outrageous conduct for a minister."

Well I read it twice...you can too, here: (**84**). It's really quite funny when it gets down to this section:

   "Until a year before the general election, he was raking in hundreds of thousands of pounds on top of his £64,000 MP's salary. He was a director of no fewer than six subsidiaries of Lazard, he worked for a City PR firm, and had a £40,000 post with a firm of management consultants. At the same time he fell foul of the increasingly tight regime over MPs' expenses. He was ridiculed two years ago when he claimed 13p for Tipp-Ex and also submitted a 45p invoice for a stick of glue.

Responding to criticism over the Tipp-Ex claim, he said: 'This is a perfectly normal office expense, the likes of which any office up and down the country might use.'
It wasn't the first time his expenses had come under scrutiny. In 2009 it was revealed he claimed £19,000 for furnishing and decorating his constituency home."

financial advisory and asset management firms, operates from 42 cities across 27 countries in North America, Europe, Asia, Australia, Central and South America. With origins dating back to 1848, the firm provides advice on mergers and acquisitions, strategic matters, restructuring and capital structure, capital raising and corporate finance, as well as asset management services to corporations, partnerships, institutions, governments, and individuals".

Have a poke around the site. They do okay and the board is pretty heavy duty.

which is registered in jolly old London. It appears to be worth

The Rest is Silence:

"that terrifying, approaching dawn, that keeps me awake is very close at hand now"

6th October 2012

I had a week away, before coming back and writing about the wolf at the gate. The rest was, well...restful. I needed it, having been at this since April. What I didn't need, was to lose my uninsured iPhone in a Children's haunted house. I say lose; apparently the gadget is so clever it can switch itself immediately and leave the area, never to be seen again.

For a blissful week I boarded pirate ships, leaped from rock to rock, enjoyed the feeling of sand and water on my feet and trekked through a rainforest.

After losing the phone I completely disconnected, Twitter was silent, no-one could call me; no emails, no text messages. Silence. And, in that quiet, I cleared my head and decided to turn the blog into a book.

As I recapped all I know; everything I've found out in the last six months; everything that has really made me think, made me worry about the future...more than ever I wanted to permanently document my concerns. Document how this happened; who was involved.

I wanted to make sure there was a full, written

record of the present. Much like Herodotus, the Ancient Greek historian once did.

When you put it all together, the big picture that I brought back from holiday, it looks like this:

Politicians & Government Office Holders
It is quite reasonable to think that

1) Serving ministers have extensive links to influential think tanks and their personal and corporate donors.

2) That correspondence relating to the reform of policing is being withheld from the public domain and that this correspondence may contain questionable or damaging information. The Home Office have made a number of contradictory statements, released a limited amount of questionable information and, also, some quite clear statements refusing to provide certain information.

3) That undue influence over current reform programmes and independent reviews may have been exerted by ministers and other office holders. This is clear from reports written as far back as 2007 and also in limited correspondence released by the Home Office.

4) That the appointment of the HMIC may not have been a completely transparent process and that details of that process are being withheld due to this. The Home Office have made clear publicly that it may unduly impact on their ability to effectively conduct public affairs.

5) That there is a relationship between ministers and private security providers and other providers, which causes public concern. This includes the nature and extent of the known problems with G4S around the provision of Olympic security.

6) That ministers have been subject to influence by corporations and individuals, via lobbying companies and other mechanisms. This is a concern of the Prime Minister and other MPs who are focused on the issue.

Senior Police Officers
It is quite reasonable to think that

1) There are extensive links between senior, serving police officers and the private security industry.

2) That there is or has been a culture of

consultancy payments and utilisation of other services, between serving ACPO officers and ACPO as a company and, former ACPO members.

3) That there are links between Serving ACPO officers and those directly involved in the police reform and outsourcing agenda, including direct relationships with those involved in the reform agenda.

4) That contracts with G4S have almost been entered into without an open tendering process by the use of 'piggy back' agreements, while forces did not make accurate assessments of what savings could be achieved.

Security Industry Figures
It is quite reasonable to think that

1) There are extensive links between the Private security industry. In particular between G4S, LOCOG, ACPO and the Home Office. G4S in previous year's investment events stating that they were in constant contact with Ministerial staff and Government officers.

2) The problems with the Olympic security delivery were known well in

advance. Due to the hugely intricate system of meetings, checks and measures it is reasonable to believe that it was impossible that they were not aware. As far back as May 2012 ongoing concerns relating to venue security are documented in a board minutes for LOCOG, at which attendees include representatives for all of these departments.

3) G4S has been engaged in discussions with ministers of the Home Office, Ministry of Justice and with Senior Police Officers for a number of years, with a focus on financial expansion through the provision of outsourcing arrangements.

4) G4S has utilised the services of lobbying agencies and think tanks in attempts to influence ministerial policy decisions and to expand their business operations. One well known lobbying agency has documented this within the 'blog' of one of their own executives.

5) That there was a conflict of interests between the new HMIC, the Home Office and G4S, via the legal firm White and Case, while the police reform reports were being completed.

Think Tanks and Linked Individuals
It is quite reasonable to think that

1) The Charity Commission has ongoing concerns as to whether the think tanks in question are subject to party political bias. In particular with reference to Reform and Policy Exchange.

2) It is factually accurate that charitable status provides tax benefits to both donors and the organisation.

3) Think tanks provide a mechanism for corporations and donors to gain 'access' to serving ministers and that this may influence policy decisions. There are reasonable grounds to believe that Localis, Policy Exchange and Reform are included within this. There have been numerous journalistic investigations which confirm this belief, including secret filming with offers of access being made . The think tanks themselves make a number of statements in publicly available articles about the breadth of their ability to contact ministers and the depth of their influence.

4) Think tanks receive donations and corporate membership payments from

companies that have overt financial interests in the obtaining of government contracts. Localis, Reform and Policy Exchange are included within this. This is supported by company accounts information, in both declarations and refusals to make information public.

5) Think tanks and other organisations are involved in the arrangement of events, where ministers and other senior figures, meet with corporate parties, interested in the provision of governmental contracts.

6) That restricted fund donations could be being used in order to produce guided or sympathetic reports from think tanks, including Reform and Policy Exchange.

For several months I've carried this burden around with me. Been weighted down by it, as I've tried to articulate it and share it as broadly as possible.

There is still no finger pointing, no wild calls for people to be dragged to the gallows; just a series of questions that need answers. Questions which, I can pretty much guarantee, nobody will thank me for asking or, which will continue to be ignored.

The future, that terrifying, approaching dawn that keeps me awake, is very close at hand now. The 18th of October is the day that Winsor Part 2 will be ratified (*the hearing actually spilled over and will reconvene on the 30$^{th)}$*.

If you've read in the newspapers that 16,000 officers will go, just imagine what will happen when they can all go at once; as forces struggle to save multi millions of pounds and are left with no other choice. What happens on this date will write the epitaph of the police service. As the dolphins would say:
   "So long and thanks for all the fish".

I have done everything I could. Everything. More than you may ever know but this last, getting the answers to these questions, is beyond what I can do alone. Before I finish though; one final, burn of the wick.

On the 3rd of July half of the world knew that Blair Gibbs would be going to work for the Mayor, as a policing advisor. (**85** & **86**). He got the job (**87**) but, I am now told, there were over 50 applicants and, that the closing date for applications wasn't until the 4th of July 2012. There is a detailed Freedom of Information request on the issue (**88**).

He had the job, it appears, before all applications were even evaluated. This is yet another clear symptom of a disease, grating so loudly on all that is good and decent, that it's causing ears to bleed. In fact, it seems that there is quite a tight relationship with senior police officers in London, which goes back at least as far as May 2012. I found this last out, having been directed to page 12 of the published hospitality register for that month. (**89**). Note it says "maintain close working relationship".

I have said many times that the Winsor Reform to policing were little more than a mechanism to introduce financial control and political interest. I maintain this. I can see a future where the police become the Orwellian boot that stamps the human face forever. This final move smacks of absolute puppetry. So much control that I have coined a new word to describe it; Orvillian.

For the first time ever, I can honestly say: I hate that duck.

You needn't look too far to find just how many of the other birds I have written about have come home to roost.

Nick Herbert left parliament in the reshuffle. It seems my assessment of his anger levels was pretty good as he is widely reported to have left in a strop (**90**). As I understand it he headed straight for the countryside, where Badger culling is now back on the menu. I rather fancy Bill Oddie's chances.

Herbert, incidentally, was replaced by Damian Green, who has immediately launched his bid to support ACPO in using drones to patrol the British skies (**91**), due to cuts to police helicopter units. It is moves like this, on top of everything that has happened so far, that have driven the Police Federation to move towards a ballot; for employment rights for police officers.

The largest bird to roost, so far, was in fact a turkey. The G4S Olympics debacle. Forces immediately backed away from privatisation deals (**94**) and then...went straight back to them, once the potato cooled down a little (**95**).

PCC elections are now fast approaching and it seems my concerns back in June were fully justified. The Electoral Reform Society and journalists are really quite concerned about the elections becoming a low turn out farce (**92** & **93**). The Home Office even went as far as trying to support the process with mailshots, via a £3 million additional spend. But as this left out independent candidates, it just fueled what I had pointed out about party politics (**96**).

Well...I did say.

Looking inward, at the police service, the horrendous revelations from Hillsborough have now been laid bare. What I saw made me sick, despite the fact I was a child at the time (**97**). Senior officers seem to have ordered that evidence be changed. In particular evidence from the front line that was critical of the police leadership or, management at the incident. Restriction of the voice of the front line appears to be alive and well in the present too. ACPO guidance was written in July and was released in August, relating to officers talking about police reform. It was designed to deal with PCCs but is worded in such a way – see paragraph 13.3 - that officers can't speak full stop (**98**). In fact, officers had no choice but to stay away from a Guardian debate on Friday the 5th of October 2012, because of this. The debate was about police morale on the front line. The situation is utterly ridiculous, but then, I had already called it 'the politics of the impossible'. In fact, the timing of that ACPO guidance comes after Nick Herbert demanded

privately for officers to be stopped tweeting.
I wrote to him, on the very topic. In June.

'I told you so' is, to me, no compensation but at least I have had the balls to say what I have said; the commitment to spend every spare, waking second documenting what was happening; trying to make sure that people knew. Trying to do something about it. But, there is hope. This week I have seen the police and the public standing together, in two very different places, in two very different and distressing circumstances. There is hope. Even in darkness.

I have burned my own little candle at both ends and, for now, I have no words left. Nothing that will suffice. So, I am borrowing those of Ezekiel; they are the only ones I can find that feel right:

"The path of the righteous man is beset on all sides by the inequities of the selfish and the tyranny of evil men. Blessed is he, who in the name of charity and good will, shepherds the weak through the valley of darkness, for he is truly his brother's keeper and the finder of lost children".

The rest is silence.

Epilogue:

"My last thought a sour 'at least'. No comfort"

1st of May 2034

The screams rose into a guttural, animal like shriek, then were replaced by a more palatable, gargling rasp; as the vocal chords burned away and the man's head caught fire. The flaming body underneath it stopped making forward steps, knelt and fell forwards with a dull thud.

"Shit!" shouted Tom in the quiet street, the only real noise the sound of human fat, softly spitting as it cooked.

He had a nice smile, Tom. Subject to many a compliment, by many a woman; and he wore it broadly as he stepped toward the charring lump. The straps of his flame thrower tanks creaked as he leaned slightly forwards, lifting the visor of his police helmet. He spat on the body and it sizzled. He laughed to himself, spat once more and turned around.

The bullet struck him clean on the bridge of the nose, driving through his face, splintering bones as it battered into his skull; mushrooming and changing direction before tearing out of the back of his head. Eventually coming to a dead stop, against the impact attenuating Kevlar, of the inside of the helmet.

He made no sound, no shrieks. He just fell backwards, as if in a faint, his pack hitting the floor with a clang, the hose rupturing at the joint, fuel spilling and running on the camber of the road. It crossed the few feet to the burning corpse in seconds. Tom exploded seconds after that, a much bigger fireball lighting up the street. Pieces of him clattered and splattered across every nearby surface, some alight, some smoking. Some raw.

In that flash I could see my reflection in the remaining half of a shop window. The black clothing, black armour, black helmet, black boots. The gun in my hand, dropped by my side. The pale, almost bright white face, behind the perspex visor. I could see a ghost.

I'm glad I shot him. Tom. He'd been enjoying this too much lately. With each new generation it seems that they have become more equipped to deal with this. I will never be able to deal with it because I remember how things were. How they should be still. I'm getting too old for this and Tom, a probationer in old-speak, was just at the beginning. By the time he reached my level of service what on earth would he be prepared to do? As I did on many a turbulent night, since it all changed, I found myself wishing more than ever that I had had the balls to do something about it; in the there and then.

I stepped closer to the window, in the grim here and now, my choice hovering over my soul like a vulture and, as the fire died back down, I saw that it had been a book shop. Nothing much there now, most of it taken for winter fuel; nothing but a carelessly torn section of a book, wedged under a breeze block. Presumably that which had broken the glass, whenever it had happened. In whichever violent demonstration or burn zone cleansing it had been done.

I don't know what possessed me to do it but I reached through, tossed the block aside and picked up the tattered pages, barely held together. I recognised the text and my heart skipped a beat. George Orwell. 1984.

I looked up and down the now deserted and long destroyed street; Bloomsbury was barely recognisable in comparison to how I had first seen it. The remnants of twenty two years of rioting and increasingly violent control. The husks of burned cars still littering the pavements where they had been repeatedly ploughed, by armoured police vehicles, in the early days of the changes. When people realised what was happening and tried to stop it. Too late. Too little, too late.

I had once thought all of this would happen.

Once called the whole situation Orwellian. I had however, like many others, not said it too loudly; nor done anything about it. I'm as guilty as the architects of this.

I'd forgotten the feel of a book, paper being as rare as it now is and found myself squeezing those tattered pages a bit too tightly. I could feel my finger tips digging in. I couldn't let go, couldn't ease up. A Fifty-Four year old copper, stood in a burn zone, with a gun in one hand and less than half a book in the other. It felt like the very last piece of the past, the last tangible thing. The only thing I could grasp at. The circling vulture squawked in delight, as my soul blackened a further shade.

Despite the fact it had been twenty-two years, I had an overwhelming urge to smoke a cigarette. Of course they were rarer than paper, as rare in fact as rocking horse shit these days but, the craving was strong. Intense. I holstered the gun and, with the grunt of an old and weary man, sat down on the broken glass and began to read by firelight.

"...the real power, the power we have to fight for night and day, is not power over things, but over men.' He paused, and for a moment assumed again his air of a schoolmaster

questioning a promising pupil: 'How does one man assert his power over another, Winston?' Winston thought. 'By making him suffer,' he said.

'Exactly. By making him suffer. Obedience is not enough. Unless he is suffering, how can you be sure that he is obeying your will and not his own? Power is in inflicting pain and humiliation. Power is in tearing human minds to pieces and putting them together again in new shapes of your own choosing. Do you begin to see, then, what kind of world we are creating? It is the exact opposite of the stupid hedonistic Utopias that the old reformers imagined. A world of fear and treachery is torment, a world of trampling and being trampled upon, a world which will grow not less but more merciless as it refines itself. Progress in our world will be progress towards more pain. The old civilizations claimed that they were founded on love or justice.

Ours is founded upon hatred. In our world there will be no emotions except fear, rage, triumph, and self-abasement. Everything else we shall destroy everything. Already we are breaking down the habits of thought which have survived from before the Revolution. We have cut the links between child and parent, and between man and man, and between man and woman. No one dares trust a wife or a child or a friend any longer. But in the future there will be no wives and no friends. Children will be taken from their mothers at birth, as one takes eggs from a hen. The sex instinct will be eradicated. Procreation will be an annual formality like the renewal of a ration card. We shall abolish the orgasm. Our neurologists are at work upon it now. There will be no loyalty, except loyalty towards the Party. There will be no love, except the love of Big Brother. There will be no laughter, except the laugh of triumph over a defeated enemy. There will be no art, no literature, no science. When we are omnipotent we shall have no more need of science. There will be no distinction between beauty and ugliness. There will be no curiosity, no enjoyment of the process of life. All competing pleasures will be destroyed. But always -- do not forget this, Winston -- always there will be the intoxication of power, constantly increasing and constantly growing subtler.

Always, at every moment, there will be the thrill of victory, the sensation of trampling on an enemy who is helpless. If you want a picture of the future, imagine a boot stamping on a human face -- for ever."

Crying I tossed the tattered pages into the dying embers that had once been Tom and took my pistol from its holster, placed it under my chin.

Pulled the trigger. I had done nothing when I could have. I hadn't taken a stand. My chance to provide a solution had died and, with it, any chance of my own redemption. My last thought a sour 'at least'. No comfort.

At least I would no longer be part of the problem.

This is not the End.

Working? Be safe.

Home? Be happy.

Wherever you are; stay lucky.

Thank you for reading.

JP.

Printed in Great Britain
by Amazon.co.uk, Ltd.,
Marston Gate.